TRAVELS
with Rainie Marie

Patricia Martin

HYPERION PAPERBACKS FOR CHILDREN
NEW YORK

First Hyperion paperback edition 1999

For information address Hyperion Books for Children,
114 Fifth Avenue, New York, New York 10011-5690.

1 3 5 7 9 10 8 6 4 2

Library of Congress Cataloging-in-Publication Data:
Martin, Patricia (Patricia A.)
Travels with Rainie Marie / Patricia Martin.—1st ed.
p. cm.
Summary: Twelve-year-old Rainie Marie, whose father lives in
a distant state and whose mother is struggling with depression,
fights to care for herself and her five brothers and sisters
and to keep them all together.
ISBN:0-7868-1339-3 (pb)
[1. Family problems—Fiction. 2. Brothers and sisters—Fictional.]
I. Title
PZ7.m364165Tr 1997   [Fic]—dc20 96-20005

FOR ROBERT
—P. M.

CHAPTER
ONE

When Mama's special friend, Mr. Sugar, died, I was the one who had to tell my brothers and sisters. At twelve, I was the oldest and often in charge. Especially when Mama had dark days.

Mama was going to miss Mr. Sugar. He had made her laugh. Mr. Sugar owned the apartment building where we lived, and he lived in the apartment two floors up. When Mr. Sugar came down to visit, he brought bacon, sometimes, and apples. In the springtime, he brought shad straight from where he had caught it in the Hudson River. He and Mama would clean it and cook it. We would all sit on the stoop out in front, stuff our faces with shad, and laugh at Mr. Sugar's jokes.

"What goes up when the rain comes down?" Mr. Sugar would ask.

"What? What?" we would scream.

"An umbrella!" Mr. Sugar would laugh, and we'd groan and laugh with him.

I looked at Mama now, sitting in her straight wood chair and staring out the window at the stoop where she and Mr. Sugar used to visit. Mama was a tiny person, except for her big eyes. They were deep as two black holes in outer space, and when you looked intently into them, you felt like you could fall in. She wore her hair tight against her head. Her sweater clung tightly to her thin body, and her skirt hugged her all the way to her ankles. Since she got the news about Mr. Sugar, she looked even smaller, like a balloon that got pricked with a pin. She had dressed herself all in brown—the color of sadness. Mama sat still as a brown stone, the lemon tea I had made her untouched on the floor.

I was the Mistress of Magic. I owned a magic acorn that gave me special power. I could put my fingers on a problem, any problem, and my magic would shoot out of my heart and down my veins and out my fingertips and into the trouble. Whenever Mama had dark days, I asked her, "Would you let my magic fingers touch you?" But Mama never let me put my fingers on her. She would always say, "Magic, shmagic! Show me cash!"

So on the day Mr. Sugar died, Mama just sat alone and untouched, and looked out the window. Once in a while, she'd sniffle and put her hands up to her temples. She'd say, "My head is full of bees, Rainie Marie."

I left Mama and walked down the short hallway. I stuck my head through the thick, raggy curtain of my brothers' bedroom doorway and called, "Samuel, I need your help."

Samuel sat on a stack of colored, cut-up crepe paper. He was cutting and pasting a collage picture and trying to keep Kenneth and Baby Eddie from eating the scraps. They often ate things they shouldn't, and then they were sorry for it later.

"What do you want, Rainie Marie? I'm busy!" Samuel was always busy when he thought he was going to have to do something.

"Make sandwiches. We have to catch the train for Beacon."

7

From the thunderclouds in Samuel's eyes, I knew he was going to explode.

"You mean we're going away again?" asked Samuel, slapping his hand onto the pile of papers. Some of them flew up into the air.

Kenneth and Baby Eddie stopped scrambling in the scraps, all eyes and attention.

"Yes," I said through my teeth.

Samuel scowled even deeper. "For how long?" he asked.

I shrugged my shoulders.

"But school!" Samuel shouted.

"So? You'll only miss one day of school and then it's winter recess," I said.

"Yeah, but . . . ," started Samuel.

I interrupted him with a shout, "Go complain to Mama!"

"Why do we have to go, anyway?" Samuel whined.

I was tired of his yelling and whining, so I blurted, "'Cause Mr. Sugar died this morning. That's why! And 'cause Mr. Sugar told Mama if he dies, this building's gotta be sold! Mama's gotta find us a new place to live! And a job! And Mama says, 'How can I think with all you kids?' So that's why, you . . . you . . . *thing*!"

A mouthful to say, and the minute I said it, I felt bad. This was not the way to tell the boys such sad and scary news. Samuel's mouth dropped wide open, but nothing came out. Kenneth put his palms together, like he was praying. He rolled his eyes toward heaven. Baby Eddie looked at his brothers, stuck his fingers in his mouth, and bawled at the top of his lungs.

Oh, brother, I thought, this was all I needed.

After I quieted the baby, I let the boys get ready. I went around the apartment, putting our travel sacks together. I had developed a very economical way to do this, since we began our travels long ago. For each of us, there was a brown paper grocery sack. Mama saved these from the times we went food shopping. Into each sack I put clean underwear and socks, a toothbrush, and a penny for luck.

While I packed, I listened to the rumble the boys made as they got ready for this travel.

The boys shared a bedroom at the back of our apartment. They slept together in one big bed. This was a cozy arrangement in the winter, but it was sweltering in the summer. I knew, because I did the same with my little sisters, Louise and Little Belli. Summer nights, we felt like turkeys on the roast, and the cook forgot to baste us! But winter, as I said, was cozy.

Our room was down the hall. Louise was watering her spider plant, which sat in the bedroom window overlooking the 7-Eleven across the street. The spider plant's spiky leaves waved under the drops of water that splashed on them. Little Belli sat on the floor, rocking Brown-Bear and crooning him a lullaby.

I told the girls about Mr. Sugar. I decided to skip the part about the search for a new home and maybe a job. Enough bad news was more than enough.

The girls took the news bravely. Tiny tears sparkled on Louise's curly eyelashes. Little Belli watched quietly. That was what she did with the world, Little Belli. She would never have ulcers or nervous breakdowns. She would just sit, calm as ice, and watch me handle the problems. I would have all the ulcers and nervous breakdowns in the family.

I put my arm around Louise's shoulder. She sniffled and snuffled. She wiped her nose on her hand and wiped her hand on my leg.

"Hey!" I slapped her hand away.

"Why did he have to die?" asked Louise. Little Belli listened, all ears.

I said, "I think maybe God needed him in heaven."

I remembered Mr. Sugar's crinkly smile and his bright eyes that smiled even more than his mouth did.

Mama liked to say, "His smile's contagious."

"Onc-cages, onc-cages!" Little Belli would agree, although she had no idea what she was talking about.

Mr. Sugar smiled even during his sick time that made him so skinny and weak. He smiled especially when he saw Mama and me walk into his apartment with plates of food. I knew he wouldn't eat the food. He was always throwing up. But it made Mama feel better.

"Lord knows, I'm not any doctor. But at least I can keep the patient fed," Mama said. Sometimes I thought she had no idea how sick Mr. Sugar really was. I knew, and Mr. Sugar knew. But Mama seemed to go through the whole thing like she was in a dreamworld.

Sometimes I thought maybe deep down she did know and just refused to admit it, even to herself.

"You wait till the shad start running in the springtime, Mr. Sugar," Mama said. "You'll be running right with them, sir."

Mr. Sugar would smile at Mama and then look at me. His smile would fade, just a little.

Louise tugged on my shirt, yanking me back to now.

"Will they let him tell his jokes in heaven?" asked Louise.

"Sure. They love to laugh in heaven," I said. "Now, go to Samuel. He will tell you what to wear for the train."

Louise and Little Belli snickered at me because I had no patience with choosing dresses. They ran into the boys' room.

I heard the boys yell. They were getting dressed and the girls had caught them with their pants down.

"Don't you know how to knock?" Samuel asked them.

"How do you knock on a curtain?" Louise answered. Louise always has an answer.

I stood in front of our mirror, which had lost most of its silver. Only the bottom corner of its right side was clear. Since I was tall, I bent down to see my face. I rubbed hard with my fingers at the freckles that covered my nose, trying to get rid of them. It never worked, but I always did it, anyway. Freckles on your face are a poor thing. Freckles were one thing my magic could not erase.

I put barrettes of different colors in my hair. Gray days could use colorful barrettes. Then I went to warm up Mama's lemon tea.

When Mama had bad days, I made her pots of lemon tea and rubbed her shoulders. Then there were times I had to take me and my brothers and sisters away. Sometimes, we just went over to Aunt Pludy's apartment. We got to play with our cousins. But there were many cousins, and Mama said, "When you think you've worn out your welcome, you'll have to come home."

Other times, we went to Aunt Cassandra's in Mahwah, New Jersey, or to Aunt Castina's in Connecticut. Aunt Castina was Mama's oldest sister by ten years. She did not have children, and she treated us like the china dolls that she kept around her house. She cooked Brussels sprouts and made you eat them all. Mama listened to her like she was Boss of the Universe. Aunt Castina was Aunt Awful, in our book.

When we were lucky, we got to go to Great-Gran Gardenia's in Beacon. Great-Gran was Mama's grandmother, and she had lived in the same house for many, many years. It was to Great-Gran's house that we were to travel now, while Mama had her dark days over poor Mr. Sugar.

Everyone lined up in the kitchen, ready for the cold walk to the train station. Samuel, who was eleven months younger than I was, was red-cheeked and very round. Then came Kenneth, who was eight. The only round thing about him were his glasses. He had taken to wearing one of Mr. Sugar's ties at all times. And his Bible was always with him, tucked under his arm.

Louise came next. She was seven and in second grade. She had black eyelashes that curled up and dark curly hair that hung way down. Her knees were always cut and bruised. Louise cradled her spider plant in her arms. It was wrapped in lots of plastic bags from the food

14

store. This way, it would not get frostbite.

Little Belli was three and a half and she had hazel eyes and wispy hair that never stayed in its braids. It stuck out all around her pudgy face. She had her bear tucked into her sweater, so she looked fat. She had two heads—a girl head with a tiny button nose and a bear head with a big fuzzy snout.

Sitting on the floor in a huge puddle was Baby Eddie, who had turned nineteen months last Sunday. We were having a problem potty training Baby Eddie.

"Your turn to change him," I said to Samuel.

"I'll give you a hundred extra raisins in your sandwich if you do it," Samuel said to me.

"There's no raisins in the whole apartment! Who can afford raisins?" I spat. Samuel could really bust my buttons.

Samuel sighed and put down the picnic bag that held the sandwiches he had made. He picked up dripping Baby Eddie. Then he sidled up to Kenneth. Kenneth grasped his Bible close to his heart, as if to protect himself against soggy diapers.

Samuel whispered, sweet as a tangerine, "Kenneth?"

Kenneth looked hard at the refrigerator.

Samuel took a deep breath and said, real whiny, "Pleeeeaaaasssse?"

Kenneth was a sucker for politeness. He put his Bible on the table. Taking Baby Eddie, Kenneth mumbled, "Do unto others, I guess."

Louise said, "Do unto others? You want Baby Eddie to change your diapers, Kenneth?" Louise never knew when to stop. "Hang on to your diapers, Baby Eddie. You don't know what you're getting into!"

The others laughed. I *tsked*, to remind them that I was the mature one.

As we waited in the kitchen for Kenneth to return with Baby Eddie, I thought about this new travel. I prayed that this travel would be our last. And I hoped that this time, somebody would hear that prayer and say, "OK."

CHAPTER
TWO

Although I had no patience deciding what the little ones wore under their coats, I was the one to get them bundled up for cold weather. I wrapped each one in extra pants, sweaters, jackets, scarves, and hats. None of us had boots, so we wore thick wool socks over our shoes.

"Can't move my arms none!" cried Little Belli.

"Aw, you're always whining," said Samuel.

I told Samuel, "Be patient for a change." To Little Belli I said, "At least you'll be warm. Would you rather move your arms or be warm?"

She sniffled. Since she couldn't bend her elbows to wipe her nose, I wiped it for her with a piece of Samuel's pink tissue that had wafted out to the kitchen.

"Mama, we're ready to go," I called. We waited. "Mama?" I called again.

Mama's bedroom door creaked open. She floated into the kitchen, silent and pale as a ghost. She smiled a weak smile and said, "What would I do without my Rainie Marie?"

I looked at Mama. "We don't have to go, Mama. We could stay here. I'd take care of all the little ones." I looked at her hopefully. I pictured me, Mistress of Magic, willing Mama to say, "Yes, Rainie Marie. Stay. Stay home forever. You never have to travel again. You won't even have to leave the house for school. We'll get you a home tutor!"

Mama hesitated. Now was my chance to save us from another travel.

"I'd take care of you, too, Mama. We all would, wouldn't we, guys?" I asked the little ones.

"Huh?" they asked.

"We'd take care of Mama, wouldn't we?" I asked.

"Sure."

"I guess."

"I'll help."

"Rainie Marie'll take care of us all," they scattered their comments together.

Mama said, "N-no. I think I really need this time. I mean, I really want you here with me, but there's so much to think about. So much to do . . . funeral arrangements, and . . . and other things." She looked at me. Earlier, remembering how Samuel and Kenneth and Baby Eddie reacted to my outburst about Mr. Sugar and moving, I had told Mama, "We can't tell Louise and Little Belli about the move yet. Enough is more than enough."

Mama agreed with me.

Now she started to cry. "There's so much to think of. Poor, poor Mr. Sugar!"

My eyes got tears in them, too. If only I could make her see that families should see trouble through together.

"Go, Rainie Marie. Your aunt Castina says the best place for you all is Great-Gran's. Don't forget, Great-Gran's the one always helped my own mama through bad times, when I was even younger than you."

"Yes, Mama," I said. I swallowed back my tears and turned to leave.

As we filed to the door, Mama handed us the travel sacks I had put together.

I led us out the door and down the steps to Main Street.

Mama called to us, "You look like a family of ducklings!" as we waddled, bundled up, down to the street. Each of us carried a travel sack in one hand and a special belonging in the other. Little Belli had her special belonging, Brown-Bear, tucked into her clothes, so she carried my travel sack for me. My arms were filled with Baby Eddie.

Every person in my family had a special belonging: Samuel had his collage stuff, Kenneth his Bible, and Louise her spider plant. Little Belli had Brown-Bear, and Baby Eddie had his fingers, which he liked to suck until they were all pruny. My special belonging was a tree that grew in the park behind our apartment house. It was a big old oak that sent down acorns every fall. The tree's roots kept it at home always. Not a bad idea!

Last fall, I picked up an acorn and put it in my pocket. I kept it there always. It kept me good company. If I was worried about a math test, or an ogre under my bed, I would rub my acorn. It grew shiny, like a diamond inside a caramel. Now—since my oak tree could not go anywhere—I traveled light with my acorn and hoped for the best.

We passed the Plug Nickel Bar, Mad Hattie's Wig and Hat Shop, Lylla May's House of Infinite Beauty, and the Caribbean Foods Store. When we came to Professor Strange's Tea Garden, we walked quickly and didn't look into the dark windows of the storefront. If you looked in, you might be doomed.

My friend Natasha once told me, "They practice mysterious magic in the back. And they make rice from cats' claws and noodles from the tails of rats."

Louise said that Professor Strange cast her teacher under an evil spell, and that was why the teacher acted like a witch. She really *was* one!

Samuel said once that he had sneaked down there and peeked in the window in the light of a full moon, and he had seen that the jars on Professor Strange's shelves held the ears of goats and of lizards.

"Lizards don't have ears," I said.

"That's because Professor Strange has got them all! So that's how much you know, Miss Smarty Booger Face!" That's what Samuel said to me.

"And maybe Professor Strange took your brains, and that's why you're so stupid!" That's what Louise said to Samuel. Louise always had to get in the act.

"An ounce of prevention is worth a pound of ears," said Kenneth, who didn't want to be left out.

All along the way down Main Street to the train station, Samuel picked up pieces of paper and plastic that looked right for his collages. Main Street had lots of litter on it, so his collages were filled with interesting and colorful items. He liked old cigarette packs the best, because of their clear, bright colors.

"Just so long as you don't use what's *in* 'em," Mama warned Samuel.

We were a proud family, in that none of us smoked. Great-Gran's husband, Great-Stepdaddy Flowers, died because cigarettes gave him cancer. So we were a healthy family of nonsmokers. That's what Mama told everyone she met. "We have never fallen into addiction," she bragged to everybody who listened.

"Hurry, Samuel!" I had to remind him that we had someplace to go. He bent down and picked up a crumpled, empty turquoise cigarette pack and ran to catch up.

At the end of Main Street, there was a steep hill down to the train station. The hill was icy, and Little Belli slipped and fell on her back into the snow along the side of the pavement. She did not hurt herself, but because she was wrapped and bundled like a mummy, she couldn't bend her knees or her arms to get back up.

Louise laughed and shouted, "She looks like a turtle stuck on its back!"

This made Little Belli squeal. She beat her stiff arms and legs back and forth in fury, making herself look very much like an angry turtle.

"This is all I need," I said. I grabbed her hand and yanked her upright.

Our procession got back on track. As we made our way over the icy patches covering the parking lot of the station, Louise skipped up to my side. She squished both her spider plant and her travel sack in one arm and tugged my sleeve.

"I know a secret," she cooed up at me. She cocked her round head in her own proud-of-myself fashion. When Louise thought she knew something, her gray eyes got silvery.

"So what's your secret?" I asked.

She bounced on tiptoe to whisper in my ear, "We're maybe going down to Daddy's in Tennessee soon."

I stopped in my tracks. *What?*

The others behind weren't watching. Samuel plowed into me, and Kenneth plowed into him. Little Belli skidded onto her back once more.

Louise smiled slyly.

"Where did you hear that?" I asked. I held Baby Eddie so tightly in my arms, he squirmed and whined.

"Mama on the phone with Aunt Castina, right before we left," said Louise.

Louise could smile and gloat about this. She had never been down there. But I remembered Tennessee only too well.

My father was a very nice man. His name was Emile Swan, and he traveled around a lot, like us. Except he went by himself. He traveled for his jobs. He did all kinds of things. Once he worked on a boat where they caught tuna fish. Then he worked in a prison. He made sure the prisoners behaved themselves. Daddy even worked at playing the guitar in a band in Nashville, Tennessee. Mama said we couldn't go to see him in his band. The place where he played had chairs with no backs. Mama said, "Too uncomfortable. Whole crazy thing's too uncomfortable for me."

Daddy led an interesting life.

"Too interesting," said Mama.

My father had done many things. And he understood the language of hummingbirds and he knew where club soda got its name.

Daddy lived out in the countryside of Tennessee. His house sat in a tiny, deep valley all his own. Everybody's house sat in one of these tiny valleys. You'd go along the big road and all of a sudden the side would drop off and you'd look way down and there would be a little white house with a white porch and pale smoke curling out of its chimney. Like a lump of sugar in the bottom of a green teacup.

But at Daddy's, the weather was always hot and sticky, even at Christmas, and you never got to go to school because Daddy forgot, or would be too late to register you, or something. Then you got put a year behind when you came back home. Just ask me; I knew for certain. That's how I ended up two times in ugly Mrs. Stanley's third grade, and that's how I ended up in the same class as Samuel. That was a terrible two years! The year Samuel and I were together, facing Mrs. Stanley morning after morning, Samuel would say, "She sure is mean!" looking to me for help just because I had had her once before.

"Yup. She puts the 'ug' in ugly, Samuel," was all I could say.

I asked Louise, "Is this travel to Daddy's a certain?"

She just shrugged. Her long eyelashes grazed her cheeks as she closed her eyes. She said, "If Aunt Awful says so, it's so." Then she bounced back to her place in line, no longer interested in the conversation.

Good old Aunt Awful, I thought. Boss of the Universe. Boss of Mama.

I plodded toward the brass and glass double doors of the train station, not caring if the others followed. I stared hard at the sidewalk under my sock-covered shoes. It wasn't until Louise yelled that I looked up.

"Snow! Look, everybody, it's snowing!"

Oh, brother! This was all I needed.

My science teacher told us that snow insulated things. Dogs caught in snowstorms dug holes in banks of snow. They crawled in and the snow kept them warm through the night. A thick blanket of snow kept warmth in the ground and protected tulip bulbs and daffodil bulbs. It made their winter sleep warm and their winter dreams sweet.

But snow was not making me warm *or* sweet. It was making a travel I did not want to take even worse than it already was.

Other kids got to *play* in the snow, I thought to myself. I got to go away in it!

CHAPTER
THREE

We huddled in the great cave of the train station lobby. Samuel scouted out the right track for our train to Great-Gran's in Beacon. I watched out the tall, tall windows. The snow came down in giant bundles. The wind blew it around in snow tornadoes. The windows rattled when the wind beat against them. I shuddered.

"Track 13," Samuel said as he came back to us.

Kenneth said, "Track 13! Thirteen is a bad number. Thirteen is evil! Thirteen is . . ."

"My lucky number," I interrupted. "As Mistress of Magic, I always have an exceptional day on the thirteenth of every month. And I will be in seventh grade when I am thirteen. And I will have thirteen children when I marry!"

I lined my little family up. Kenneth was not going to put fear of numbers into them. Especially since I didn't totally believe everything I'd said, and wished that instead of track 13, we were on track 9 or 4 or 2,100,345! Anything but 13!

There were sixty-four steps from the station lobby down to the train platform. I counted them out loud. That would teach the little ones their numbers.

The conductor, who puffed out his chest and seemed proud of his blue uniform, helped us up the huge steps onto the train.

We took up two rows of seats. We had one row on the river side, which the sisters took. We had another across the aisle on the city side, which the brothers took.

The train rumbled and roared as it jerked to a start and rolled slowly, bumpily along the tracks into the snowy world between our city of Poughkeepsie and Great-Gran's city of Beacon. It dipped and swayed, and I feared we'd roll right over into the cold, gray Hudson River.

Being in charge is a big responsibility, but it is also a helpful thing. Being in charge of a family keeps your mind off fearful things, like people dying and people moving; like snowstorms, trains on track 13, and trains that tip into the water. And it keeps your mind off pictures in your head, like the picture of Mama all alone in our apartment, sitting still as a stone. Supervising the unwrapping of the little ones from their coats and scarves and hats was a chore that I didn't mind, not at all.

After everyone was unwrapped and our wet coats were stashed on the floor under our feet, I sat back and watched the snowstorm beating away at the Hudson River. I wondered: Would we ever stay in one home long enough to grow roots like my oak tree back home?

I reached deep into my pocket. My acorn was there, all smooth and safe. I looked over at Louise and Little Belli. They chewed on their fingers and giggled, completely unconcerned about anything.

"Get your fingers out of your mouths," I snapped at them.

"What's the matter with you, grouch?" asked Louise.

"G'ouch!" copied Little Belli.

I sucked my teeth at them and went back to my worrying.

The boys, on the other side of the train car, pointed to snow mounds in the meadows. They looked like they didn't have a care in the world.

To put my worries away, I took count. I started on the girls' side. There was me, and there was Louise, and there was Little Belli. And on the boys' side, there was Kenneth, and there was Samuel, and there was . . .

"Where's Baby Eddie?" I called to Samuel.

"Right here," Samuel said, and he continued to gape out the window as if he'd never seen a snowflake in his life. He pointed his finger to where Baby Eddie had been, but to where now there was an empty space.

"Right where?" I asked. My voice was shrill and made Samuel and Kenneth and the girls swing their heads around. We stared at the empty Baby Eddie spot on the seat.

Louise, never at a loss for words, said, "Uh-oh."

At once, we all jumped up and yammered at one another.

"Where is he?"

"Where'd he get to?"

"Not under there . . . not here . . . where?"

"Maybe he's playing hide-and-seek," suggested Kenneth.

"Uh-oh," Louise said again.

Both Baby Eddie and Little Belli often played hide-and-seek. They'd just go off and hide and not tell anyone. They hoped that sooner or later they'd be missed and then found.

I said, "If he's doing that on the train, and if we don't find him in time, we could miss our stop!"

"Miss Beacon?" cried Louise.

"Miss G'eat-G'an?" cried Little Belli.

I said quickly, "Now, don't get all upset. We'll find him, is all."

"Let's call the conductor," suggested Samuel.

"No, we can handle this." I didn't want the conductor to think that I couldn't take care of my own family. And I didn't want to bother any of the passengers. They might never let us on the train again. Then what would we do?

I said to everybody, "Get down on your hands and knees. We'll find him. He's got to be crawling around somewhere in this car."

We got down on our hands and knees. The floor was grimy and yucky. Louise and I tried to let only the heels of our hands and our knees and the tips of our toes touch the floor. Little Belli loved the idea of crawling and swished herself all around.

"*Psst!* There he is!" Samuel called to us in a loud whisper. We looked to where he was pointing. Sure enough, on the floor under a seat, I saw a round little bottom covered in bulky green pants, and round little feet covered in dirty white socks.

Louise called, "Baby Eddie!"

"*Shhhh!*" I told her. "He probably doesn't want to be found!"

I was right. Baby Eddie dipped his head down under the seat and saw that we were on the chase. He giggled and skedaddled.

I tried to follow Baby Eddie's trail. I would see the soles of his feet disappear behind one seat and then his dirty, chubby fingers reappear in front of another seat. He crawled fast in and out of the aisle, back and forth between the spaces in front of the seats, over strangers' feet and between their ankles. The rest of us crawled just as quickly after him.

As we passed each seat, the passengers looked down at us and frowned. No one asked us what was wrong. By now, I wished they had. I was getting scared. Baby Eddie was always two crawls ahead of us, and always out of reach!

In a minute, I realized that I had a *reason* to be scared. Baby Eddie had perched himself smack in front of the big door leading out of the train car. He leaned against it, stuck his fingers in his mouth, and slurped. Through the window in the top of the door, I could see the blue hat and pink head of the conductor. He was headed right for the door.

"*Sh-h-h!*" I put out my arm, making the others still. We stayed on our hands and knees, some of us in the aisle, some of us between the seats, with our heads peering out.

Either of two things could happen. If the door opened into the car, the conductor would slam it wide and Baby Eddie would be crushed.

If the door opened out, Baby Eddie would fall back, out onto the rickety platform and right off the train!

"Kenneth, what do you think would happen if we called to Baby Eddie to get out of the way?"

I spoke quickly; time was important!

Kenneth studied the situation. "He'll lean harder into the door, just to annoy us. You know Baby Eddie—he's another Louise." Then he pointed his finger to the ceiling like a hallelujah minister. "As the Lord said to Moses and his friends, 'Thou art a stiff-necked people.'"

"Oh, for goodness' sake, hush!" I snapped at him. I looked up at the door's window. The conductor had turned away, as if he were talking to someone behind him. Then he turned back toward the door. He reached his arm for the handle.

I turned to Samuel. "Quick! Distract Baby Eddie!" I cried as I made ready to sprint down the aisle.

Samuel charged forward like a mad rhinoceros. He grunted and roared. Several of the passengers screamed and threw their hands up. But Baby Eddie laughed fit to beat the band.

I charged up on Samuel's heels and slid in front of Baby Eddie. I swooped him up in my arms, just as the conductor jerked the door wide open. It pulled back out of the train.

Clutching Baby Eddie, I looked out to the

shaky old train platform between the cars. I blinked away a surge of tears.

The conductor looked at us, smiled, and nodded.

I did my best to smile and nod back.

As I turned to carry Baby Eddie back to our seats, a lady sitting at the front of the train said, "Oh my, what an adorable baby! May I hold him for a while?"

She looked very respectable. She wore thick glasses. On her head was a beautiful green hat with a golden feather that reached down to her shoulder. She had lots of red curls.

Since my head was aching and since I was feeling very impatient with the baby and with the whole day, I said, "Yes, ma'am." I handed him to her and made my way through the train's sway and jostle, back to my seat. I hoped that now things would quiet down.

CHAPTER
FOUR

As soon as I became comfortable in my seat, I heard a cheerful squeal from Baby Eddie. I looked up to where he sat with the lady. I saw a grubby little hand. It had the lady's big thick glasses in it, waving them around like a flag and smudging the lenses.

I heard the lady say, "Oh my, don't do that, dear. Your fingers seem to be sticky." She laughed, but it was a short, cold laugh: "Eh-heh. Eh-heh."

Then I saw the same grubby little hand reach up and grab the lady's green hat. Before I had a chance to run and keep Baby Eddie from making mischief, the little hand yanked. Not only the hat come off. The lady's whole head came off!

The green hat with the golden feather and all the beautiful red curls were swept away in Baby Eddie's little hand.

"Oh my! Oh no!" screamed the lady. She held her head, which had skinny, ugly gray hair sticking up in sprouts.

I stopped where I was, trying to hold back my giggles as Baby Eddie gurgled and waved around the green hat with its wig of auburn curls.

"You little monster!" she yelled. And then she let out a bloodcurdling wail, "Isn't this child potty trained?"

Now I ran down the aisle, trying to stay on my feet despite the jerking of the train. Baby Eddie sat on the floor where the lady had dumped him. Hat and wig on his head in lopsided glory, he clapped his hands.

I heard Louise plow up behind me with her big feet. She peered over my shoulders at Baby Eddie and said, "He gets that from *your* side of the family, Rainie Marie."

When we got ourselves resettled in our seats, I changed Baby Eddie's diapers. Changing diapers on a train requires special organization. You have to use the train seat without getting it wet.

I told Samuel and Kenneth to scrunch themselves into the girls' seat until I was done.

"You're gettin' fat," said Louise to Samuel.

"Yeah, fat!" said Little Belli.

"Well, you're both getting uglier and uglier," replied Samuel.

The girls cried, "Rainie Marie!"

I gave them my gravest face and it worked. They stopped their fussing.

After Baby Eddie was fresh and dry and everyone was settled into the proper seat, Samuel and I opened the picnic bag. We scooted around and squeezed ourselves between the seats, passing out the sandwiches. We were very glad for something to munch on.

The conductor finally came around and collected tickets from people. I gave him money and he put the tickets onto the tops of our seat backs. We thanked him very much, and he tipped his hat to us. Little Belli laughed, and the conductor put his hat on her head. The hat was much too large and slid down over her face.

This made Little Belli cry and she screamed,

"Dark! Dark!" She had no love for the dark. "You let the dark catch me!" she howled.

Little Belli's howling made Baby Eddie cry. All this noise made Samuel shout, "Shut up!"

Saying "shut up" made Louise yell, "Bad! Bad!" In school, her teacher made the class write *shut up* ten times if anyone said it. Louise never let anyone say it, for fear she'd have to write.

Louise's yelling made Kenneth reach over and pinch her legs. This made Samuel take their half-eaten sandwiches away from them. And that made them all wail like train whistles.

People wrenched their heads up high on their necks to look over the seats. They shot us their reddest glares.

"Quick, give me those sandwiches!" I snapped at Samuel. I shoved the sandwiches back into the little fists that were banging on knees and waving in the air.

"Now stop crying," I told my brothers and sisters, "or you will flood the train and your sandwiches will get waterlogged and they'll float away and so will you, right off the train and into the river!"

The little ones wiped the tears from their cheeks and rubbed their eyes. Each one gave a last huge sniffle. Then they sank their teeth into the soft white bread of their sandwiches, sighing and nodding contentedly.

The passengers on the train settled into peace and quiet once more.

We finished eating and Samuel took the others to the water fountain in back of the car. Water was a necessity after the stickiness of peanut butter. The little ones got frustrated if they couldn't wag their tongues as quickly as they liked to.

Of course, then Little Belli had to go to the bathroom. On trains, there was only one bathroom for both boys and girls. It had a gray door, the same color as the river that day.

I knocked on the door and checked the little round circle under the handle. It said VACANT so I took Little Belli inside.

When we returned to our seats, Louise, who had apparently been sitting and thinking, asked, "Where's the poop go?"

"What?" I whispered sharply.

"When you go on the train, where's the . . . ," Louise began again.

"I heard. I heard," I said, holding my forehead with my hand.

Samuel leaned over from across the aisle and said, "It shoots out a pipe onto the train tracks."

"Gross!" said Louise.

"It does not," I said.

"Does so," Samuel insisted.

"How do you know anyway, Mr. Know-It-All?" I asked.

"Your friend Natasha told me," Samuel said.

"Made it up," I said.

"No!" he insisted.

"Yes!" I insisted back.

"Did not!" Samuel yelled.

I sighed and turned toward the window, deciding to ignore the whole thing.

"So there," I heard Samuel say under his breath.

After he turned to stare out of his window, I poked Little Belli with my elbow. I whispered, "Don't believe it."

But Little Belli hissed into my ear, "Does so!"

The children's eyes that had been wide as full moons turned slowly to half-moons, then to slivers of moons, and they drifted off to sleep.

To help them get there, I sang them this song:

The moon will always glow for me,
The stars will twinkle in my pocket,
I'll serve Sir Mars some lemon tea,
And fly to the sun in a silver rocket.
Until then I'll just say good-bye
And go eat my apple pie,
Which good Great-Gran has baked for me,
Which good Great-Gran has baked for me.

I looked at all my little brothers and sisters. Samuel slept with Baby Eddie asleep in his lap. Samuel's collage bag was tucked neatly between his knees. Kenneth clutched his Bible to his heart, even in his sleep. Louise had propped her spider plant up in the corner of the seat, so its fronds tickled her cheek and made her scratch her face while she was sleeping. Little Belli cuddled her Brown-Bear and nuzzled her nose into its stuffed belly.

"Beacon! Station stop, Beacon!" The conductor's words woke me up; I hadn't realized I'd been asleep.

"C'mon, c'mon, all you! Wake up. Quick! We don't want to miss the stop." I clapped my hands and got everyone moving.

My brothers and sisters opened their moon-eyes, yawned greatly, and waited to be wrapped for the cold. Samuel helped me, as we had to beat time.

I looked out the window. Night had crawled in while we were asleep. The snow still fell like great scoops of puffed-rice cereal. Beacon's street-lights glowed like ghosts through the fluffy flurry of snow.

The train slowed and sighed with relief. We lined up in order down the aisle of the car. Samuel had Baby Eddie in his arms. The baby was still sound asleep, his head lolling on Samuel's shoulder. Baby Eddie's mouth gaped open and a thin line of drool made a dark spot on Samuel's tan coat. Baby Eddie was snoring to beat the band.

"He's drowning out the train," said Louise.

"He's having the sleep of angels," said Kenneth.

"Some angel," said Louise.

"Do angels drool?" asked Little Belli.

"Hush up! Now!" said Samuel, in his usual bad humor.

I didn't say anything. Like the train, I just sighed.

CHAPTER
FIVE

The train door hissed open and the conductor stepped down the big metal steps. He turned back to the train to help the passengers off. I took count of my ducklings.

"One, two, three, four, five . . . all here," I said.

"All here," they answered.

"If you're not here, raise your hand," I said.

Little Belli raised her hand and Samuel asked, "Oh, you're not here, huh, Little Belli? Then where are you?"

We laughed; Little Belli is fun to catch. She sucked her teeth and pulled a face, but then she grinned.

The conductor said, "Come along, come

along, easy now." He held up his hand to help us down. Getting off the train took us a while.

We plowed through the swirling snow into the train station lobby. It was empty, except for some people who were meeting passengers that rode to Beacon with us. A man whose red plaid jacket was covered with glittering flakes of snow hugged the woman with the green hat and red wig-curls. He took her bag from her, cupped her elbow with his hand, and led her out. On her way through the door, the lady looked back at us, hunched her shoulders up close to her neck, stuck her nose way in the air, and said, *"Humph!"* Then they disappeared into the snow swirls.

The other passengers left the station. Echoes of feet and shutting doors bounced off the stone and marble walls, then faded to nothing. It became quiet.

There was just us.

"Where's Great-Gran?" asked Samuel angrily. "This kid is getting heavy."

"Well, sit down on the bench over there," I said, and he did.

Kenneth walked over to me, grasping his

travel sack and his Bible so tightly that his knuckles were pale, shiny balls.

"Rainie Marie, where's Great-Gran?" he asked.

I swallowed deeply, trying to get the panic to stay inside so I wouldn't upset the little ones.

"The snow probably held her up. Don't worry," I answered him.

I ushered them over to the long, dark bench in the middle of the station lobby. I told them to sit quietly and to reassure them, I said that I would ask the ticket seller for information. My brothers and sisters sat stiff and wide-eyed, watching me and watching the door.

I went over to the ticket window, keeping my eye on the little ones. I got to the ticket window and saw that it was shuttered. A yellow paper with black printing said, WINDOW HOURS, 6 A.M.–5 P.M.

I stood very still and tried to think. My thoughts got mixed up with my anger. If Mama didn't send us away all the time, this would never have happened. If we were a normal family, like the families on television, this would never have happened. What were we, Gypsies?

I decided then and there that I would never let my own family loose like this. We would stick together, thick as honey—*and no more traveling!*

But this thinking did not help us out now. I put on my all-in-control face and sauntered back to the bench.

No one said anything, but they looked at me with questions brimming in their eyes like tears.

"Nothing to worry about," I said. "Great-Gran will be along any minute. The snow has held her up. I'm sure of that. Great-Gran has never let us down."

Little Belli's lower lip quivered; then her nose quivered and she started to cry. Louise put her arm around her and said, "When has Great-Gran ever let us down, Little Belli?"

Little Belli looked up at Louise through her tears.

"And when has Rainie Marie ever let us down?" asked Louise.

Little Belli turned to look at me.

"Thank you, Louise. Now, we will sit here and wait calmly," I said. "Great-Gran always comes through for us. That is her job. That is what she is best at."

We sat with our backs straight as ironing boards. None of us owned a watch. We could not tell how much time passed. The big clock high up on the station wall said one o'clock. Its hands had never moved in all the times I had been there. A broken clock did not tell you much.

Outside, the black of the night was alive with swirling cyclones of snow. No cars moved; no people came.

I had to do something. I felt in my pockets. In one pocket, my precious acorn. In the other, a flat, round object. I pulled it out. A nickel.

"Does anybody have any money?" I asked.

All the brothers and sisters felt around in their pockets. Together, we had one nickel, one dime, thirteen pennies, and one quarter. Phones don't take pennies, so I had enough to make only one call.

"You gonna call 911?" asked Kenneth.

"That's just for sick people or burglars in your house or babies with their feet stuck in toilets, stupid," said Louise.

"Is not!" said Kenneth.

"Is too!" said Louise.

"Who you going to call?" interrupted Samuel.

"I don't know yet," I answered him over my shoulder. I was already heading for the line of pay phones against the wall.

If I called Great-Gran, I was taking a chance. She might not be home. She might be on her way here. A phone call to her might not make sense, since she knew we were coming.

A call to 911 might make the 911 people mad at me. None of us was sick or being robbed or stuck in a toilet.

A call to a taxicab company might make better sense.

Great-Gran or a taxi or 911? I decided to flip a coin. Heads, it would be Great-Gran; tails, it would be a taxi. If it landed on its edge, 911. I took a dime, then decided to flip a penny. If I lost the dime down a heat register, I would have ten less cents. If that happened to a penny, I would have only one less cent.

The penny went up into the air. It looked black against the pale gray walls of the station. It looped in the air and fell and hit the floor with a *ping*. It rolled in three circles and then settled onto its side.

Tails. Call the taxi.

The first phone booth had no phone book. I went to the next phone booth. No book. I tried to think of Great-Gran's number, in case there were absolutely no phone books in the station. I knew I knew it, but it had disappeared through some crack in my brain.

I went down to the last phone booth. There was a tattered phone book dangling from a chain. I opened the book to the taxi services and called the one that I knew Great-Gran used. It was the Sunyellow Cab Company. We needed some sunyellow about now.

A man answered. "'Lo?" His voice was gruff and unfriendly.

"Hello. Will you please send a taxicab to the train station?"

"What train station?" he asked.

"The one in Beacon," I told him.

"Hey, you sound like a kid," he said.

"I am a kid," I admitted.

"This a joke, or what? We get plenty joke calls," he said.

"No, sir! This is no joke," I assured him.

"Yeah? Well, your voice sounds too familiar

51

to me. You called here before, didn't you? Sent my cabs on wild goose chases!" he accused.

"No, sir! I didn't! You have to believe me!" I pleaded with him. If he refused me and hung up, I did not have any money left for any more phone calls.

"Next time you kids call, I'm gonna sic the cops on ya!" he shouted at me and slammed down the phone.

I had to face the others with my failure. I walked slowly back toward them, not looking up. I didn't want to see the disappointment on their faces. I didn't want them to see it in mine.

"Rainie Marie Greene?" a tall man in a yellow coat called. He came striding in through the door, out of the snow.

"Yessir!" I called back.

"You got a great-grandma Gardenia Flowers out on Oldhome Road?"

"Yessir!" I yelled, my heart bursting with relief.

"Got a cab for you." He showed me his official taxi-driver identification card. "Let's go!" he said.

* * *

On the slow, slippery ride to Great-Gran
Gardenia Flowers's house out on Oldhome
Road, I had many thoughts. I thought my old
angry thoughts about my family's resemblance
to Gypsies. I thought stern thoughts about being
a mother duck with a string of ducklings to care
for. And I thought that a person always needed
a person, someone to depend on.

Warm and dry in the taxi, I still longed for
Mama and home. Second to that, I longed for
the coziness of Great-Gran's and for the famous
hot chocolate Great-Gran always had ready for
us. Her hot chocolate was the best in the world.
She melted big marshmallows on the top, a half
marshmallow in each mug of chocolate. If you
were real good, you'd get a whole marshmallow
all to yourself. I could almost smell the steaming
chocolate, right there in the taxi.

CHAPTER
SIX

We drove slowly through the streets of Beacon, but they looked like the streets of heaven. The snow-covered trees were giant angel feathers tickling the pale night sky. The road was a cloud and the air glimmered like thousands of angels had just flown through, kicking up diamond dust.

The cab crawled around a curve onto Great-Gran's street and crept on in silence. We passed a house that stood in the storm dark and empty-looking. And another house, just as dark. And another. Was anyone home on Oldhome Road?

And then we came to a house whose windows had warm yellow lights glowing. As the taxi rolled to a stop, the house's front door opened. A woman—a dark, thin silhouette against the light behind her—stepped out onto the porch.

I reached over and threw open the door of the taxi. We piled out onto the street, climbing over a bank of snow.

"Great-Gran! Great-Gran!" we shouted, clambering up the slippery wooden steps.

"G'eat-G'an!" cried Little Belli, sliding and flailing her arms.

Light glinted in Great-Gran's glasses as she tossed her head back and laughed. She bent down and bundled us all to her.

"A sight for sore eyes, you surely are!" she exclaimed.

She led us through the door into a warm yellow living room that smelled of hot chocolate.

Louise exclaimed, "You made us Great-Gran's famous hot chocolate!"

"Yay! Yay!" the little ones cheered, jumping and clapping their cold, red hands.

"Something even better," said Great-Gran, helping me take the hats off Baby Eddie and Little Belli. "Guess who made a special trip to Beacon, just to help me welcome my great-grandchildren!"

"Who? Who!" demanded the little ones. I had a sneaking suspicion that I did not want to know who.

Great-Gran continued to tease. "And who do you think is out in my kitchen, making her own very special recipe of hot chocolate?"

"Who?"

That's when I heard sharp footsteps stabbing the hallway floor, tattooing their way toward us.

And Great-Gran announced, "Here she is, your favorite aunt Castina!"

With that, the doorway darkened. A huge figure stood on the threshold, gripping a tray of mugs. Aunt Castina barged in like a steamroller on high heels. She stomped across the room, casting her shadow over us. As a group, we shivered.

Little Belli drew in a sharp breath; Kenneth clutched his Bible to his chest. Samuel took a giant step back, toward me. Baby Eddie leaned over and threw up.

"Yikes!" exclaimed Louise. I didn't know whether she said yikes at the throw-up or at Aunt Castina.

"Rainie Marie . . . ," Great-Gran started. She didn't have to finish her sentence.

"Yes, ma'am," I said. I ran to the kitchen, slipping a little in the thick wet socks I still wore over my shoes. I grabbed a bunch of paper towels and ran back. I got on my knees and cleaned up Baby Eddie's throw-up. It was only a little. I went into the bathroom and threw the mess into the garbage.

When I got back, Aunt Awful shoved the tray of mugs under my nose.

"Hot chocolate?" Her offer rumbled like a ball of thunder. She grimaced, trying to smile. How could she think we wanted her terrible concoction now, while we were still in our coats, dripping melted snow onto the floor? But when Aunt Castina offered, we had to be polite. We each took a mug of the lukewarm stuff.

"That's my great-grandchildren," said Great-Gran. "Now, drink it down and get warmed up. Then we'll get you all settled in."

"This stuff wouldn't warm up a fire!" said Louise, who was the first to try a sip. *"Yuggghhh!"* She made an ugly face.

The little ones looked at me.

I bent my head toward my mug. It was cold. I took a sip. My mouth puckered itself almost inside out. My tongue glued itself to the roof of my mouth. Yuck! I looked up at Aunt Castina. She smiled her fierce smile, looking very pleased with herself.

"You like it?" she asked, all smiles and

grimaces. "Carob sugar-free cocoa. No caffeine, no sugar, no—"

"No marshmallows!" cried Samuel, interrupting our aunt.

"No taste, neither," cried Louise.

I saw the look on Great-Gran's face. I thought for sure that we were in for a lecture. But she didn't say anything. She picked up a mug in a grand gesture and took a large swallow. She gulped. Her face turned greenish and then reddish. Her eyes watered, and she coughed.

I wondered if Aunt Castina was trying to poison us. And I also wondered if Aunt Castina was here to stay.

After we choked down Aunt Castina's awful cocoa, Great-Gran swept us through to the kitchen. Her three black-and-white cats, Kit, Kat, and Cynthia, snuggled together in front of the warm oven. They raised their glossy faces, peered at us with eyes that were sleepy and green, yawned, and resnuggled into themselves.

Great-Gran rubbed our cold, red feet with thick towels and told us, "When the snow got so bad, I knew I couldn't make it to the train station. Luckily, your aunt had driven up here from

Connecticut when she heard the sad news about your mama's Mr. Sugar. She wanted to help. Your aunt and I are cooking your mama lots of food, and Castina will drive it up to Poughkeepsie tomorrow. She'll take good care of your mama."

I'm sure she will, I thought. She'll boss Mama around like nobody's business. I hated the fact that Aunt Awful would take over my home, when I wasn't even allowed to be there.

Great-Gran continued, "We decided to call the taxi, because even Castina didn't dare go out in this storm. And the Sunyellow Cab people are people I can trust. They'd keep you safe as beans, children, safe as beans!"

I decided that someday I would tell Great-Gran that the Sunyellow Cab people hung up on me, but not right now. I was in too much of a hurry to get warm, and I was too tired.

Aunt Castina swept into the room and ordered, "Rainie Marie, hang these coats and things on the backs of chairs along the heat registers. Now, please."

Then she said, "I'm going to bed. I've had a long day. Good night. And make sure you wash those mugs out, Rainie Marie. The hot cocoa will stick, you know."

"Yes, ma'am," I mumbled.

I put all our sock-boots in a basket for washing and mending, and then warmed some milk on the stove for a batch of real hot chocolate, Great-Gran's famous recipe.

Great-Gran supervised the putting away of clothing and toothbrushes. Samuel opened the sofa bed in the living room, Kenneth opened the sleep-chair in Great-Gran's bedroom, and Louise helped make up the double bed in the extra bedroom.

We let Great-Gran's famous hot chocolate warm us, and then we went to bed. The little ones only grumbled a little; we were all weary from our travel.

I shared the sofa bed with Samuel whenever we visited Great-Gran. After Great-Gran had turned off the lights and gotten herself tucked in, I lay in the dark. The moon wasn't winking in tonight; the snow clouds kept its silver to themselves.

Houses had a way of telling you all about who lived inside. Walls mirrored dreams; floors echoed laughter and tears. Maybe it was the spirit of trees in the wood that made wooden houses. Maybe it was the spirit of earth in the bricks that made brick houses. Whatever spirit it was, it sang clearly. A person could hear it, if a person took the time to be silent and to listen.

Great-Gran's house sang in the winter wind. Great-Gran said its dark wood creaked because it was old and full of voices of the dead.

"People have died in this old house," Great-Gran said. "Some died happy, some died sad. And some died, but forgot to stay that way."

Even if there were ghosts singing in the walls, it was a friendly house. In summer, the thin white curtains in the living room danced in the breezes from outside. In winter, the house smelled like cinnamon and warm bread and chocolate.

I listened to the sleep sounds in Great-Gran's old house. In the spare bedroom, Louise ground her teeth and Little Belli kicked her feet. I heard the *fup-fup* of the sheets as she ran races in her dreams. In Great-Gran's room, Kenneth's sleep-chair creaked. I heard his Bible slide softly to the floor.

Aunt Castina's snores tore through the house like the roars of an elephant. Great-Gran's soft snores floated out from her bedroom. Every once in a while, she coughed, deep and heavy. The coughs sounded like they hurt. Then Great-Gran would moan and sigh, and her soft snores would come floating out once again.

Baby Eddie, nestled in tight beside Great-Gran, slurped his fingers, making wet sounds.

Beside me, Samuel's breath was soft and slow.

I rolled my acorn back and forth in my palm until it was warm. I pictured my oak tree alone in Poughkeepsie, snuggled in under its blanket of snow. I lifted the tip of my pillow and tucked my acorn between it and the mattress.

I relaxed my muscles, one by one. It was a routine I always did when sleep played hide-and-seek with me. I relaxed first my toes, then my heels, then my whole foot. Then I relaxed my legs and my knees and my thighs. I'd go up and through my entire body, letting one part after another become a sack of Jell-O. Last, I relaxed my brain and thought only of nice things—flowers and roots, nests and houses that made homes, homes that people never had to leave. And I did not open my eyes until the morning sun shining on the snow sent a joyful white light into the house.

CHAPTER
SEVEN

Great-Gran Gardenia was a singing woman—
like me. Mama said the singing trait usually
skipped one generation, but this time it skipped
two. Mama was not a singing woman, and neither was her mother.

Whenever I was in Beacon, we sang.

Sugar maples in the garden,
Tulips on the hill,
Oatmeal cookies in the oven,
Silver dimes in the till.
Nobody's gonna get us down,
Nobody ever will!

The house kept time with us. The spirits that
held the house upright also kept it in tune.

"We're in tune with the earth and sky, Rainie Marie," said Great-Gran. "It's everybody else that's out of tune," she added, and laughed. Kit, Kat, and Cynthia curled around her feet.

Great-Gran was bent over and bony. Her short curls were wispy white against her crinkly skin. Her skin was so wrinkled she said, "I got more lines on my face than a street map of Beacon! My lines are more crooked than the Pleasant Valley Road!"

Great-Gran wore round glasses with golden rims. They slid down to the tip of her nose, and she would peer at us over the shiny frames.

She slept with her teeth in a blue glass on the table by her bed. The blue glass had yellow stars painted on it. It was a beautiful glass.

Great-Gran said, "My teeth are like stars—they come out at night." She laughed and laughed, and I laughed, too.

She also kept flowers in pots and glass jars and old bottles all around her house.

"I might not always have a roast on the table, but I'll always have flowers," said Great-Gran. "It's our job to support our mother, Nature. This is my way."

Great-Gran's sheets were crisp. They smelled softly of flowers. But the sheets were white; they had no flowers printed on them.

"Colors in sheets weigh down your dreams," she said.

Great-Gran kept her dreams in a special box made of redwood, polished so that swirls of light shone from it. There was a tiny black key hidden away somewhere that kept the dreams locked safely inside. The box was on top of a bookcase in the living room, on a white scarf with pale fringe.

"My dream box. Don't ever touch it!" Great-Gran wagged her finger at us.

"Looks like a plain old box to me," whined Louise the day after we arrived. She was feeling sorry for herself because there was no television.

"Well, it isn't. It's special," I told her.

"How come?" asked Louise.

"'Cause," I said.

Louise walked over to the bookcase. She stood on her tiptoes, her chin on the top shelf, and stared at the box.

"Nothin' special about that!" said Louise.

Samuel looked up from his book called *Collages for the Young and Old*. He read it whenever he was upset or away from home. "If that box is so special, then it should look special," Samuel said, giving it his artistic eye.

Louise ran over to Samuel. She dipped her hand in the collage bag on the floor by his chair. Bits of gold and turquoise and leaf-green tissue floated from her fingers onto the dark denim that covered his knees.

"Don't have to look plain, not with you around," she said.

"Better not touch it," I warned.

"But now's a perfect time for Samuel to fix up the box, as a surprise for Great-Gran. She's busy with Aunt Awful, cooking for Mama. She won't be out of the kitchen for hours," said Louise.

"Nobody wants anybody fooling around with a special belonging," I said, "which is what Great-Gran's box is, her special belonging—"

I was interrupted by an unearthly roar that was coming from the spare bedroom. Samuel, Louise, and I jumped a foot into the air.

Screeching! Hissing! Yowling!

"*Ya! Ya! Wah!*" I heard little voices shout.

"*Meeeewwwwlllll!*" I heard screeching voices howl.

Samuel cried, "Little Belli and Baby Eddie are at the cats again!"

"Kenneth is in there. He'll take care of 'em," Louise said.

We both looked at Louise, curled our lips, and said together, "Right." I got up and followed the squeals and screeches into the bedroom.

Kenneth was seated in a chair, silhouetted in the winter light of the window. He had a *Lives of the Saints* picture book open in his lap and was reading. He acted as if there wasn't a thing in the world that could disturb him.

"Kenneth! What are you doing? Don't you hear that mess?" I asked, exasperated.

"Mess?" he asked. When Kenneth finally came out of his trance and saw what was going on, he took off for the living room in a split second.

I looked at the shivering clump of blankets and hands and feet and tails writhing in the middle of the bed. It seemed as though the bed were trying to eat whatever came near it. The pale yellow flowers on the wallpaper seemed to shake on their stems. Great-Gran's house was sensitive to strife.

"Little Belli," I called. I heard her muffled wailing under the blanket. I scrounged around and straightened both knotted sheets and knotted tails.

Out came Little Belli with a tear-streaked face, a naked Baby Eddie, and the three cats with different parts of them stuck in something white.

"What is this?" I shouted over the hubbub because Little Belli and Baby Eddie were still wailing.

"Di-dey," said Little Belli. Diaper, she meant.

"What!"

"I changed the kitties, but only one di-dey. So I put all the kitties in one di-dey."

I picked up the pile of cats caught up in a tangle of disposable diaper. The glue on the tags of the diaper stuck to their fur. They cried and howled like banshees on the night wind. They scratched, too.

"That is very naughty, Little Belli. You mustn't put diapers on cats. Cats are not cut out for diapers, and diapers are not cut out for cats," I said.

"But I put the kitties on the potty. They fell in! Those kitties are not potty trained! Bad like Baby Eddie!"

"That is not what potty training is," I said. "Kitties do not use the toilet! Kitties go to the bathroom in their litter box, or they dig holes outside. Now, let's get Baby Eddie into a clean diaper, before we are really sorry," I said.

"Can I help?" asked Little Belli.

"Sure," I said. Little Belli is a good girl. She just tries too hard.

By the time I got the cats out of the one diaper and had Baby Eddie into another, he and Little Belli were ready for naps. I tucked them both in tightly and went back to the living room. The cats disappeared, finding dark corners to hide and sulk.

"Samuel!" I cried when I got to the living room and saw what had happened there. "What have you done?"

Great-Gran's special box certainly looked special now! Samuel had transformed it with a collage of the moon and stars.

"It is in honor of Great-Gran's teeth," he said.

Under the moon was a blue-white cloud, and there were zillions of silver stars. A golden angel flew in front of the cloud. She was playing a golden trumpet.

Louise grinned from ear to ear. "I'm going to get Great-Gran," she announced, and flew into the kitchen before I could stop her. I didn't know if Great-Gran would appreciate us changing the look of her special belonging.

When Great-Gran came into the living room, pulled by her apron by an excited Louise, her face turned pale. She clasped her hands tightly under her chin.

Samuel took a giant step and huddled next to me, as if for protection. I put my arm around him; he felt tense and stiff.

"And did you all happen to look inside the box?" asked Great-Gran. Her voice sounded funny, as if her words were boxing one another on the way out.

"No, ma'am. It's locked," Samuel squeaked.

"Yes, of course; I forgot," said Great-Gran. She cleared her throat several times.

I thought, maybe Samuel should have pasted some gardenias on it. Maybe he should have honored her name, not her teeth.

Great-Gran took a tiny step toward the box. Her fingers plucked at her lips.

Kenneth clutched his *Lives of the Saints* book tightly to his chest like a shield. He stepped toward Great-Gran, saying, "Samuel has not buried his talents, like the men in the Bible. Today he used them, just for you."

Great-Gran Gardenia squinted her eyes at Kenneth. She squinted at her special box covered with its starry sky, and then she squinted long and hard at Samuel. Her gaze returned to her box, and her lips curved into a big, wide grin. Great-Gran picked the box up and examined it closely. "Well, then, I'll love it to death!" she said.

Samuel breathed a great breath; tension gusted out of him like a north wind. Kenneth let his book fall onto the chair behind him. He walked to Samuel and patted him on the shoulder. They grinned at each other. Louise gurgled over Great-Gran's now-fantastic box, counting the stars. I ran to Great-Gran and gave her a hug. The wood of the floors and the plaster of the walls hummed with happiness. We were back to normal again—or as normal as a traveling family could expect to be!

Great-Gran disappeared, with her box, into the back of the house. My brothers and sisters settled into their own comfortable spots. I went to the window looking out onto Oldhome Road. I admired the snow clinging to the trees.

I wished that I was home, so that I could creep under my oak tree. I'd tell it about Great-Gran's special belonging and about her humming floors and walls.

I talked to my tree a lot, when I was home. I told it important secrets. I'd climb up into the tree and lie back along a long thick branch. I'd eat apples there and toss the cores onto the ground. They would be dinner for raccoons and possums. I thought of summer nights in my oak tree. If I sneaked there in the middle of the night, would I see raccoons and possums sitting together, eating my apple cores? Would I see squirrels joining in, nibbling at acorns? Would I see a wonderful wilderness feast?

This summer, when we were back with

Mama and settled in a new home, I'd do it. I'd climb on my branch and wait, silent as a leaf. I'd wait under the moon and see the wilderness feast in the night's silver light.

When I thought of our new home, it was a pleasant thought. Maybe we'd each have our own bedroom, or at least our own bed. And the boys would have a door on their room! I felt sure our new place would be close to the old place. Mama did not take to change well and would not want to move far. New things and new people scared her.

Suddenly my pleasant, sunny thoughts were overshadowed by something dark and sinister. I didn't know exactly what this dark shadow was. I scanned my filing cabinet of a brain and found it, this dark shadow. It was Tennessee.

Suppose Louise was right? Suppose we, or some of us, were to be shipped off to Daddy's? Suppose Mama couldn't find a new place or a job? Suppose Aunt Awful convinced her that we should live in Tennessee, while Mama stayed in New York?

If I was home in my tree, its strong, scratchy branches would make me feel better. Those branches and that tree were there to stay. Forever. Trees have roots. Roots were the thing to have!

I wished that Mama was here. I wished that Mr. Sugar were here, also. The afternoon air was filled with impossible dreams and wishes.

Then I thought of Samuel's work. His dream had changed a plain wooden box into a beautiful universe.

Maybe dreams and wishes aren't impossible! Maybe I can dream Tennessee away. Maybe I can dream Aunt Castina would go to Tennessee, and then I can wish her *and* Tennessee away, right out of our lives! I thought to myself.

I was jarred out of my thoughts by Aunt Castina's voice, which filled the air like the roar of a grizzly bear. She burst into the room and announced, "Now that you're all settled, I'm going to take this food and drive up to your mama. She needs me."

She needs *me*, I thought.

I watched Aunt Castina shrug her huge self into her huge dark cloak. Aunt Castina never wore coats, like normal people. She wore cloaks, so she could shrug into and out of them and swirl them around to look like a queen. When she walked through a garden in one of her summer cloaks, she swirled it so much it chopped all the heads off the coralbells and the daisies. Today, as she walked down the snowy pathway to her car, she made the snow fly off into new drifts, she swirled her cloak so.

She called to me over her shoulder, "You take care of things, Rainie Marie. And remember to do the dishes as soon as you finish eating. Food sticks!"

And she drove off in a whirl of cloak and snow to Poughkeepsie—to where I belonged.

I remembered last night's dark thoughts. Would Mama listen to Aunt Castina's advice? Would we all be sent off to the far reaches of Tennessee, never to go home again?

CHAPTER
EIGHT

Just before suppertime on the second day we were at Great-Gran's, I asked, "Could I call Mama?"

Great-Gran said, "Tonight, child. You can stay up late and call after nine o'clock. The rates go down then, y'know."

I hugged Great-Gran and ran off to tell the others.

"Don't make any plans for after nine o'clock," I advised them.

"Oh yeah, right," said Louise. "As if we won't be in bed after nine o'clock. As if we would be out on the town after nine o'clock!" And she sucked her teeth at me.

"Why not?" Samuel asked me.

"We're going to call Mama," I said.

"Yay!" all the children yelled.

"Now we really hung'y," cried Little Belli, who always celebrated things by filling her stomach.

Often at Great-Gran's, we cooked up a batch of pancakes for supper. We loved "breakfast for supper." Great-Gran's pancakes were sweet and steaming, with a big pat of melting butter on top, and thick maple syrup on top of that, and powdered sugar on top of that. But Samuel hated breakfast for supper. To him, it was an insult.

"A growing man needs steak," he pronounced as Great-Gran reached into the refrigerator, looking for eggs.

"Growing men want steak, growing men go get jobs to pay for steak," Great-Gran said. Her mouth was stern, but her eyes smiled through the starry glint the refrigerator light made in her glasses.

Kenneth overheard. "Pancakes are perfect for supper," he said. When he spoke *p*'s together, he punched them out like staples, spraying spit with each punch. "Bread is the staff of life, you know," he said.

"Pancakes ain't bread," said Samuel.

"Don't say 'ain't,'" said Great-Gran.

"Uh-oh," cried Louise. She had dropped the canister of flour all over the kitchen floor. It piled up like the snowbanks outside. Its dust floated, making the air full of soft, dry snow.

"This is all I need!" Great-Gran and I said at the same time.

I looked through the flour storm at Great-Gran. I waited for her to explode. But she simply put her fists on her hips and heaved a huge sigh, blowing the white air around.

Then Kit, Kat, and Cynthia discovered the good feel of flour. They leaped in it, rolled in it, rubbed their backs in it, and switched their tails like angry witches in it. They took flour baths, scratching their hides in it.

Great-Gran trudged off to the broom closet, shaking her head. Over the howl of cats wrestling in the flour pile, I heard her say, "Just waxed that creaky old floor . . . ghosts in that cellar pullin' that canister down like a magnet! Three dollars' worth of flour, gone! Too bad them ghosts don't pay rent, trouble they make!" She came back with two brooms. She handed me one, and together we attacked the flour.

Great-Gran and I were both so busy concentrating on keeping the dust down, neither of us saw what was happening behind us. I turned around just in time to see Little Belli and Baby Eddie run into the kitchen and jump into the flour pile, along with the cats. We now had five miniature snowmen, laughing and squealing and meowing and pawing one another. They kicked up such a gust of flour dust, we could hardly see each other.

Great-Gran whacked the broom into the flour piles. It was a miracle that she missed whacking the five little white behinds.

Long, long ago when I was a kid—maybe in first grade or so—our teacher read us a book called *Evan's Corner*. At least, I think that was the name. Anyway, Evan had his own special corner in his apartment. His corner had a window and a plant in it.

"What a great idea!" I said to Mama at the time. Samuel had agreed.

"Everybody needs his own territory," said Samuel.

"Her own niche," I said.

And that is what we had at home. Some of our niches were tiny spots. For instance, I had my seat at the kitchen table. It is where I kept my books and my pictures of birds. It was a spot that would always have room for me.

Louise had her window in our bedroom. If ever Louise disappeared, we knew we could find her kneeling in front of her window, looking out onto the busy city street.

We each had a spot, a corner, at home. We missed having a special spot when we went on our travels.

Samuel explained this, in great detail, to Great-Gran, the morning after the flour fiasco in the kitchen.

And so, Great-Gran gave Samuel a special fold-up table in the corner of the room she sewed in.

"This is for your artwork, Samuel. You made my special box a work of art. Maybe you can do more things, s'long's you're on recess from school," Great-Gran told him.

Samuel was delighted. "Wow! Thanks, Great-Gran," he said, already piling his material onto the table.

"Well, we just lost Samuel under that pile of scrap paper. He'll be gone forever," I said to Kenneth.

But Kenneth wasn't paying attention. Great-

Gran had pushed a comfy chair in front of a sunny window. The chair had broad flat arms.

"Just right for your Bible studies, Great-Grandson," Great-Gran said. Kenneth curled up in the chair, sitting like a Buddha on a pedestal. His Bible was propped up between his knees, leaning against his crossed ankles. A notebook perched on the chair arm. Kenneth loved to copy down favorite quotations into notebooks. He kept all the notebooks. He had a box of them in safe-keeping under Mama's bed.

"Mama will guard them," Kenneth said, long ago.

"As if anyone would want them!" said Louise.

Louise had her spider plant sitting in a big window in Great-Gran's living room. And below the window on the floor was an old wooden rocking cradle. This was for Little Belli's Brown-Bear. The girls played house in their own little corner.

Even Baby Eddie had his own place in a playpen Great-Gran always kept in her attic for new babies that came along.

I sighed and moped in circles around the kitchen, where Great-Gran was still cleaning up stray flour dust.

"What's your problem, Rainie Marie?" she asked.

"Oh, nothing," I sighed. I looked in despair at the ceiling.

"Well, good!" said Great-Gran and kept swiping at the counter corners.

I hated when Great-Gran ignored my sighs. She didn't ever dig deep to seek out my problems.

I sighed again, louder than before.

"Watch out, Great-Granddaughter. You'll be sucking in all this dust in the kitchen, and maybe some of the pots and pans, too!" Great-Gran laughed.

I dropped my chin and my shoulders and looked at Great-Gran. Her eyes behind her glasses were smiling and kind.

"Everybody has a special place here but me," I blurted out.

"Why, Rainie Marie, I love when you come visiting. There will always, *always* be room here for you."

"I know, Great-Gran. That's not what I mean. Everybody has a special corner for their special belonging. Samuel has his collage corner. Kenneth has his Bible study chair. The girls have . . ."

"Oh, I get it," interrupted Great-Gran. "Well, my dear, what special belonging do you have?"

"Well, you know my oak tree back home?" I had told Great-Gran all about it, many times.

"Why, yes." She looked out the window, her finger crooked against her lips. "I'm afraid I don't have any oaks here, but we've got a nice sugar maple."

"No, that's not what I mean. See, I have this acorn from my tree."

"Ah! An acorn. From the tiny acorn do mighty oaks grow! Rainie Marie, you get your acorn this minute. We'll see what we can do."

"Yes, ma'am! It's right here!" I cried, reaching into my pocket.

No acorn.

I tried the back pockets of my jeans. Not there, either.

"It must be in the sofa bed, under the pillow. Be right back!" I cried.

The blue sofa bed stood innocently in the living room, looking like an ordinary couch.

"Hiding my acorn, are you?" I whispered to it.

The pillows Samuel and I used at night had been put back in the hall closet. The sofa was all closed up.

"Let's see," I said to myself. "If I left the acorn under my pillow, it's probably stuck way down inside the folded-up mattress."

I flung the sofa cushions onto the floor and yanked out the bed. I smoothed my hands over the sheets on the thin mattress. No lump of an acorn there. I double-checked, then got onto my knees. I laid my head flat on the floor and squinted into the dark under the sofa.

Nothing.

Nothing around the couch, nothing under the rugs scattered on the floor, nothing under the table.

"Whatcha doin'?" asked Little Belli. She stood behind me, clutching Brown-Bear.

Louise, never to be left out of anything, stood close by. "Whatcha doin'?" she repeated Little Belli's question.

"My acorn! It's gone!" I yelled.

"Uh-oh," mumbled Kenneth, getting up from his Bible chair.

Louise ran off toward Great-Gran's sewing room, screaming, "Samuel! Samuel! Get in here!"

Samuel came running. "What?!"

"My acorn. It's gone!" I wailed.

"The cats," he said.

"Huh?" we all grunted.

"Cats ate it," he explained, as simply and calmly as if he were saying, "Today is Thursday and the sky is blue." He turned to go back to his collage making.

Great-Gran's voice came from the doorway. "Are you certain, Samuel? Cats do not ordinarily eat acorns."

Samuel shrugged. "I saw 'em nibbling away at something brown and round," he said.

I sank onto the mattress of the sofa bed. I hung my head almost to my knees. My hair dribbled across them, tickling them.

"My acorn," I groaned.

"You can always get another one," snapped Samuel. He still loitered in the hallway, eager to get back to his work.

"No," I said.

He shrugged and turned and left. He didn't understand. That acorn had been with me for so long. It was the child of my oak. I was an acorn-sitter. My tree kept me safe, holding me in her branches and giving me support to lean against. My tree shaded me from the hot summer sun in

August, gave me her sweet green leaves in April and her golden leaves in October. She was a mother oak. I had had her child in my pocket. Now it was gone. Into the cats' stomachs.

Great-Gran went off toward the kitchen, calling, "Kit! Kat! Cynthia!"

Kenneth sighed and shook his head. "Rainy-day Rainie Marie." He returned to his Bible.

Louise and Little Belli hugged me, and Baby Eddie, sprawled out in his playpen, belched loud and long in his sleep.

The story of my life, I thought. One big gas pain.

In the distance, the phone rang. Great-Gran came to the living room door. "Rainie, your mama's on the phone."

"Mama!" I cried, jumping up from the couch and knocking Louise and Little Belli onto the floor. "Mama!" I picked up the receiver and burst into tears.

"Rainie Marie, what is going on with you?" she asked.

I told her in gulps between tears about my acorn.

"But it's an acorn," said Mama. I could hear exasperation finding its way into her voice.

"But, Mama, it was my special belonging," I cried.

"Later, Rainie. Don't I have enough burden on my shoulders, without worrying about some acorn? Only way I'm eating is thanks to Aunt Castina. Thank the Lord for her and the food she brought me."

"Mama, I'm sorry," I said. Mama didn't need to hear complaints from me. Not at this time of great sorrow for her.

"Your aunt Castina's been caring for me and advising me."

"I'm sure she has been, Mama."

"Your aunt Castina said I have to think of myself now. Your aunt Castina said I have to plan for my future, and that I need time alone, to pull myself together. She said she's going to help me look for a new place to live, too. And I'm desperate to find a job, Rain. I need a job. But then I have to think, who's going to care for all the little ones, when I'm working? But your aunt Castina said everything will fall into place. The Lord will provide, said Aunt Castina."

My aunt Castina sure had a lot to say.

"You agree with her, don't you, honey?" Mama asked.

"Well . . . ," I began, but Mama interrupted.

"I knew you would."

This time, I interrupted Mama. "But I don't agree! We should be there with you! Not Aunt Castina. You are our mother. We are your kids. Your future that you're planning is our future, too, Mama. Our future as a family! Do you see, Mama?"

"No, I do not see. I was sure you'd understand, but I should have known better. After all, you are only a child. You don't realize futures take money. I got no money for nothing, now. How am I going to find a place to live, find a job, and take care of all you kids at the same time? And my head aches so," said Mama.

"If I were home, I could make you lemon tea. I could rub your shoulders."

"Who'd take care of the little ones for Great-Gran?" asked Mama.

"But we'd all be home together. Please, Mama. Please!"

"Oh, Rainie, I don't know. I miss you all, but I'm desperate, honey," sighed Mama. I felt maybe she could be pushed into a yes.

"C'mon, Mama. We all want to come back. Please let us," I begged.

"Do you think it could be . . . ?" started Mama.

Then I heard Aunt Castina's voice boom out of the background. She called to Mama, "You want Brussels sprouts for supper or succotash? Haven't you been on that phone long enough, with the phone bills you already got?"

"I have to go, Rainie Marie. Give me over to Great-Gran before I hang up."

"Mama, why do you always listen to Aunt Castina, and you never listen to me?"

"Please, Rain, get Great-Gran," repeated Mama.

"Yes, ma'am."

That night, my sleep was filled with dreams of Mama and home. I dreamed of my oak tree. I woke up crying.

Great-Gran was sitting on the edge of the sofa bed.

"What is it, pumpkin girl?" she whispered.

"I should be home with Mama," I whispered back.

"Don't you like visitin' your great-grandma?"

"Yes, but . . ."

Great-Gran got up and padded quietly to the

window. She pulled open the curtain. "Come over here and admire the stars," she whispered across the room to me. She coughed once but held the next cough inside.

I lifted off my covers, careful not to disturb Samuel. I tiptoed to my great-grandma. Our skin shone silver in the starlight.

Great-Gran had a practice of finding pictures in the constellations. They were not the usual pictures of dippers or bears or the great hunter, Orion. They were pictures belonging only to Great-Gran.

"Why, I believe I see a little girl picking an apple off a cherry tree," she said.

"Nobody can pick an apple off a cherry tree," I said.

"Among the stars, you can," said my Great-Gran.

CHAPTER
NINE

I woke up and scrunched my hand under my pillow, feeling for my acorn. Then I remembered. My acorn was lost forever, eaten by cats. Good grief. Grief seemed to be a family trait. I rolled slowly out of bed, wondering if I would be depressed forever. Samuel was up and gone.

"Don't tell me you're awake before I am, Samuel," I called out.

No one answered.

"Samuel?" I called again.

No answer.

"Louise? Little Belli?" I tried.

Great-Gran bustled in from the kitchen, closing the swinging door behind her.

"Finally awake, hey, sleepyhead?" she asked,

mussing up my hair even more than it already was. She coughed a little, tapping her chest with her fingers.

"Yup. Where is everybody?" I asked.

"Busy. Now you go get washed. I need someone to sweep the snow off the front porch."

"But, Great-Gran, I'm hungry. Can't I even eat breakfast?"

"You go on and get dressed and get out on that porch. It needs attention. And stay out of the kitchen," warned Great-Gran.

"Why?"

"I'm busy," she said, and she was gone.

Some "Good morning," I thought. Some "Welcome to a new day"!

I got washed and dressed and bundled up in my coat. I headed toward the kitchen. That was where the broom was kept.

Great-Gran headed me off at the swinging door. She carried the broom in her hand, and she shoved it at me.

"Here you are," she said.

My stomach rumbled, loud and clear.

"Oh, don't worry. I'm fixing you some breakfast right now. I'll call you when it's ready."

"Thanks a million," I muttered, plodding out into the cold.

Some winter recess from school, I thought. Being kept by a slave driver in Beacon.

The morning was sparkly, with the sun glistening through the icy branches of the trees. It was freezing cold. I sniffled. Freezing cold weather made me sniffle and have to pee. I swept some snow dust off the porch onto the white snowbanks in the yard. The world was still, and even though I stood in the midst of a magical crystal castle, I missed the songs of birds. I even missed the wails of my little brothers and sisters.

Where was everybody?

"Rainie, oh, Rainie Marie," Great-Gran called. I opened the door and stuck my head in.

"Yeah?" I called back.

"Breakfast is ready. Come into the kitchen," Great-Gran sounded mysteriously sweet and chipper.

I set the broom against the side of the house and went in. Not bothering to take off my coat, I stomped down the hall and pushed open the swinging door of the kitchen.

All the family was there, lined up in front of the windows that ran down two of the kitchen walls and met at the corner. Samuel, Kenneth, Louise, Little Belli, and Great-Gran stood side by side. Baby Eddie was propped up in a high chair next to Great-Gran.

"Surprise, Rainie Marie!" they called, and they parted.

Behind them, lined up on the windowsills, were shiny, dark green flowerpots. And from the pots rose twigs. And glued to the twigs were pieces of Samuel's leaf green collage paper, cut into the shapes of oak leaves.

Hung across the windows over the pots was a banner. Bits of paper and crayoned letters spelled out RAINIE MARIE'S OAK GARDEN.

"I don't believe it!" I exclaimed, walking over to examine this oak garden more closely.

Each pot had soil in it. Twigs were stuck into the soil. Oak leaves were glued to the twigs. And some of the twigs had paper acorns glued to them. Some of the leaves had tiny collage caterpillars on them. One of the miniature oak trees had a beautiful paper butterfly resting on its tip. An origami robin perched on a twig branch of another oak tree.

I turned to see them all smiling at me.

"Your own special place, Rainie Marie," said Great-Gran, gently. "In your favorite room, the kitchen. The heart of every house."

"Home of your favorite chocolate chip cookies," said Louise.

"Home of Great-Gran's famous hot chocolate," said Kenneth.

"Home of your very own special oak garden, with your very own oak treelets we made special for you," said Samuel.

"And *acorns*!" cried Little Belli.

What did I do? I turned and ran out of the kitchen, bursting into tears, leaving the door swinging violently behind me.

My heart was full to the brim with feelings, all fighting each other. My family was so good to do that for me! But I didn't deserve it. Because I didn't want their oak garden. I just wanted my old acorn back. My acorn was my magic, my special belonging, my only piece of home.

I had a wonderful family that got up extra early and went out into the freezing cold to dig up dirt and find twigs. I had a wonderful family who made me a beautiful banner. And here I was, thanking them with selfish tears. What was wrong with me?

I was in a warm, safe place with my Great-Gran. Why couldn't I call this place home?

Because the place that was home was not this place. This place was a warm and welcoming visiting place. Home was where Mama was. It was where you knew every crack in the ceiling and every spiderweb. It was where you decorated your Christmas tree and where you hid your Easter eggs. It was where you hid your turnips under your mashed potatoes and were allowed to get away with it; where you burped out loud and picked your nose; and where you could be in a bad, evil mood and take it out on your mother or your brother or your sister, if you wanted to.

That was what home was. And that was where my oak tree was.

I sat on the edge of the sofa bed, which was still open and unmade. Kit, Kat, and Cynthia were streaking around the living room, yowling and jumping on one another and playing.

I sniffled, wiped my eyes and then my nose on my hand, and then wiped my hand on the sofa bed sheet. I stood up and yanked at the sheets. Today was Friday, wash day at Great-Gran's.

I snuffled as I yanked. The cats continued to go crazy at my feet. They were after something under the couch. Kit reached and rolled something along between her paws. I heard the clear, hard sound of it spinning. I bent over and picked up the thing she was playing with.

It was wooden and round and brown. It was a catnip ball. There were tooth marks all around it. It looked like it had been enjoyed by the cats many times.

"Samuel!" I called.

Samuel came into the living room. "Yes, Miss Spoiled-Brat-Who-Cries-When-People-Do-Nice-Things-for-Her, what do you want?"

"Samuel! Look at this. Is this what you saw the cats nibbling at the other day?"

Samuel looked closely at the wooden ball I held in the palm of my hand.

"Could be," he said.

"Well, is it or isn't it?" I demanded.

"Yup. Looks like it."

"That means my acorn is still around somewhere!" I yelled.

"Yup. Looks like it," said Samuel, and he sauntered back out to the kitchen.

Almost as good as found! I said to myself.

The crisp, warm, buttery aroma of toast and bacon wafted its way into the living room. With my stomach doing somersaults and my mouth watering, I ran out to the kitchen, thanked everybody sincerely for my wonderful oak garden, and pushed a chair over to it. I sat in the midst of my paper oak treelets and dug into the breakfast Great-Gran had made for me.

Winter birds in New York State are usually brown, like sparrows, or black, like starlings. But my favorite winter bird was the color spot of the season—the fire-engine red cardinal.

One perched on the bird feeder that stuck to the outside of the kitchen window, right where my oak garden was. After I finished the breakfast Great-Gran had made for me, I sank back into the kitchen chair. I watched Mr. Cardinal peck at the birdseed in the feeder. His beak was short and rounded. It looked very sharp along the edges, perfect for seed pecking.

Peck, peck, peck. He stuffed himself full of seeds, just as I had stuffed myself full of toast and bacon.

"Peck, peck, peck. That fat little piglet," exclaimed Great-Gran, sitting across the table from me. She warmed her hands around her mug of coffee, even though it was warm in her cozy blue-and-white kitchen.

"My two little piglets." Great-Gran smiled, looking from me to the cardinal and back again.

The cardinal suddenly lifted off the feeder, spread his wings, and flew away.

Great-Gran said, "Back to the nest! Their visits never last long."

"Great-Gran," I said, "his visits are short, and then he gets to go home to his nest. Our visits"—I pointed my finger to my chest—"are long, and our stays in our nest with Mama get shorter and shorter all the time. Even the birds get to stay home more than we do."

Great-Gran took a long sip of coffee, peering at me over her mug. The steam fogged up her glasses. She took them off and rubbed them gently with the hem of the yellow sweater she wore.

"Rainie Marie, it's tough these days, for a mother with no daddy to help out. It's hard to raise kids, and keep a home, and—"

"Daddy may not be there to help, but I am!" I exclaimed.

"Maybe so, dear, but you can do only so much. And—"

"Other mothers do it alone," I interrupted again.

"We're not discussing other mothers. We are discussing your mother."

"Well, what makes Mama so different from other mothers, that she can't do it alone? Most of the kids in my class don't have both a mother and a father all the time. They make out, without traveling all over the place."

"All of them, Rainie? Are you sure? Does your class end up in June with exactly the same kids as it began with in September?" asked Great-Gran.

"Well, maybe not. But—"

"And do all mothers get along just swimmingly, with no help?"

"Well, maybe not. But—"

"But we are talking about your mama, and none of the others, aren't we, dear?" asked Great-Gran gently. I nodded my head.

Great-Gran placed her glasses firmly on her

nose and took another sip of coffee. She shifted herself in her seat, cleared her throat, coughed a rumbly cough, and reshifted herself.

"Rain, let me tell you something. Your mama was the baby of her family. Castina was born first, as you know. Then Cassandra, then Pludy, and then your mama. Castina was only seventeen when their mom got really sick. That left Castina in charge. Well, she had been in charge for a while, anyway. Like you, Rainie Marie. And when their mom died, some five years later, well, Pludy and Cassandra and your mama were just used to listening to Castina." Great-Gran paused and sipped her coffee again. It had cooled a little and did not steam up her glasses anymore. The fragrance of the coffee floated to my side of the table. Coffee always smelled so good and tasted so evil.

I said, "Wait a minute. You just said Aunt Awf—er . . . Aunt Castina was . . . like me?"

"*Mm-hmm,*" she nodded her head and smiled. Her eyes danced. "Just exactly like you. She started caring for her younger sisters when she was just a youngster. Like you. She had a forceful personality. Just like you. And she had love as big as the universe in her heart, for her family. Just like you. Surprising, you being so much like . . . Aunt Awful!"

There's a thought, I thought, glowering. Then I felt my face turn hot and red.

"You know about how we call her Aunt Awful?" I asked.

"I have twenty-twenty hearing, Rainie."

"Twenty-twenty hearing? Oh, brother!" I giggled.

"Well, dear, at any rate, your mama had been used to being the baby of the family. Castina did everything. Castina made all the decisions. She did all the work. And Castina enjoyed it. She was good at it. Like you are, Rain. Now, understand, I love all my granddaughters equally, much as I love all my great-grandchildren. But I see what I see. Castina can be a bit domineering."

"You can say that again!" I said.

"All right. Castina can be a bit domineering. And your mama can be, um, easily led. Life often seems to overwhelm her."

"But why does she have to do everything Aunt Awful says? Aunt Awful says us kids should go live with Daddy in Tennessee. She just wants us to disappear, so she can have Mama all to herself!"

"That's not true, Rainie Marie. You've got to realize, you are your aunt Castina all over again. You think you know what's best for the family and Castina thinks *she* knows what's best for the family. You and Castina, Castina and you . . . peas in a pod, if you ask me." Great-Gran stopped and swigged down the rest of her coffee in a great gulp.

Oh, brother, this was all I needed. Me and Aunt Castina, Aunt Awful and me. Were we really so much alike?

Great-Gran got up and took her coffee mug over to the sink. She rinsed it out. Did she do it because Aunt Awful had maybe said to her, "Coffee sticks, you know"?

I looked out the window for the cardinal. Where was he—snug in a nest in some nice oak tree? Home?

CHAPTER
TEN

After I'd finished my breakfast, I cleaned up. I heard the phone ring over the sound of running water in the kitchen sink.

Great-Gran stuck her head in through the kitchen door. "Rainie Marie, it's for you."

I threw the dishrag into the soapy water. "Is it Mama? Is it Mama?" I shouted.

"It's your aunt Castina."

I stopped dead in my tracks.

"Oh," I said.

Some people have a particular talent. That talent was to be in everybody's business all the time, and even from long distances. My aunt Castina had that talent. Did I have that talent, too?

"Rainie Marie! Rainie Marie! Are you there?" I heard the shrill, tinny sound of Aunt Awful's voice blaring out of the telephone receiver, clear across the room. I trudged over and picked it up.

"Yes, Aunt Castina. Here I am," I managed to say without sighing too deeply, or crying, or screaming.

"Good news! I got you a job for while you're in Beacon. Aren't I something?!" announced Aunt Castina.

"Huh?"

"A job. A job. A neighbor of Great-Gran's. Mrs. Shanty Sacs. You know her?"

"Aunt Castina . . ."

"Mrs. Shanty Sacs's got three kids."

"Aunt Castina?"

"And you're their new baby-sitter!"

"Aunt Castina!"

"Congratulations, Rainie Marie."

Mrs. Shanty Sacs lived across the street and down from Great-Gran's house. She wore glasses with fake diamonds in the frames and leopard-skin pants and high, high heels and tight purple velvet tops. She had red hair that was clumped on top of her head like rotten tomatoes. And she had three brats.

She brought them over the day after Aunt Castina told me her "good news."

"Well, here are my little angels," Mrs. Shanty Sacs said, between gum snapping and bubble blowing.

Great-Gran *tsked* at her. Great-Gran hated gum chewers, and especially hated gum snappers.

Mrs. Sacs's angels stood in a line from little to big. Not that any of them was big. The biggest was a little boy, about as big as Little Belli. The medium one was a little girl, about as big as Little Belli's Brown-Bear. And the smallest was a tiny boy, about as big as Kit, or Kat, or Cynthia. But they weren't babies, Mrs. Sacs's angels. They were older than babies. They were just baby built. As if she fed them nothing but baby food and they never grew up.

And they turned out to be bogey-babies that tortured me all day!

There they stood in the kitchen, in ragged jeans and filthy T-shirts and with their hair sticking straight out like clumps of straw. All three were chewing gum to beat the band, a-snapping and a-chewing and a-blowing their bubbles, in exact time with their mother.

Chew chew snap chew
Blow blow snap
Chew chew snap chew
Snap snap snap

"My Lord in heavenly days, save me!" exclaimed Great-Gran.

Mrs. Shanty Sacs snapped and blew and smiled a big grin at Great-Gran. "Angels, ain't they, Mrs. Gardenia Greene?" she asked proudly, blowing a huge bubble and popping it so it flung itself in a pink sheet over her nose and down her chin. Her thick tongue licked and prodded the gum back into her mouth.

"My Lord in heavenly days!" Great-Gran repeated. She shook her head and removed herself to another room, letting the swinging door swing shut behind her.

"I just know you're all gonna have some fun," Mrs. Sacs called over her shoulder, on her way through the back door. It seemed she couldn't get out fast enough.

I called after her, "But Mrs. Sacs, maybe we should talk!" I reached out and grabbed at her arm but missed.

"Talk?" she asked, screwing up her face as if she'd never heard of the word.

"Yes. Maybe this is a mistake. I have my own family to watch—"

She interrupted. "Just the point, Rainie Marie.

While you're watching all them, what's a few more? Your aunt Castina said, 'Rainie Marie is perfectly capable.'"

"But—"

"Your aunt Castina assured me. Bye!" And she was gone as if a magician had waved his magic wand and whisked her away.

I turned around to face the three angels. They were snapping and popping and blowing their brains out. They were also pushing and pinching and tugging one another. The littlest boy tugged the arm of the girl. The girl pinched the littlest boy and at the same time punched the big boy in the gut. The big boy pulled the girl's hair so hard, a clump of it came out in his hand. The girl screamed a loud and shrill "*Yeeeeeeek*" and pushed the little boy so hard, he fell flat on his hind end with his feet flung up in the air. He screamed a loud and shrill "*Yiiiiike!*"

In the meantime, Little Belli, Baby Eddie, Louise, Kenneth, and Samuel tiptoed into the kitchen to see what the commotion was. Louise shouted above the screaming, "Do something, Rainie Marie!"

"Yeah, do something, Rainie Marie!" shouted Kenneth and Little Belli.

The Sacs brats stopped squalling and looked at me. "Yeah, Rainie Marie, do something!"

And they all started moving in, slowly and surely, coming at me.

Rainie Marie, Rainie Marie,
Do something, do something,
Rainie Marie.

They chanted and inched closer and closer. I saw the image of Aunt Awful's face floating above them all. I could almost hear her crooning,

Rainie Marie, Rainie Marie,
Perfectly capable
Rainie Marie!

What could I do? I yanked the back door wide open and hurtled down the path, following in Mrs. Shanty Sacs's wake.

"Hey, man! Hey, man!"

"Rainie Marie! Rainie Marie!"

"Hey, man! Hey, man! Let's play hey-man! *Yeouch!*" The screams followed me all the way down the path, skating across the frozen winter air.

What could I do? I turned around. As I trudged back into the house, I thought to myself, For the second time in two days, I've run away from something and then come back. I've never run away before. What is happening to me?

We spent the day this way: my own sisters and brothers hid away in their special corners and peeked out from behind books and dolls and green leaves and pieces of paper. They watched Mrs. Sacs's angels zoom around the house, screaming, "Hey, man! Hey, man!" at the top of their lungs. I would make the angels stand in a corner. They would stand there for maybe five seconds, and then they would take off, once again zooming around the house and screaming, "Hey, man! Hey, man!" Those angels gave me a headache, and headaches were not my friends.

When Mrs. Shanty Sacs finally came to get her angels, and I couldn't even hear them anymore, I collapsed in Great-Gran's favorite chair. "Samuel," I called to my brother. "Bring me a wet rag for my head."

"OK," Samuel said.

I sat up and looked at him. "OK? Just like that? No argument?" I asked.

He smiled at me. "If anybody deserves a wet rag, it's you, Rainie."

"Never mind a wet rag. I've got something better," Great-Gran said. She came through the door into the living room with a tray in her hands. I started to get out of her chair, but she said, "You stay right in that chair, miss. It's the best in the house." She stooped down and put the tray in my lap. On it was an ice bag for my head and a teapot.

"Nice hot lemon tea. Just like you make for your mama," said Great-Gran with a smile.

I smiled back, leaned back, and let myself be served. Louise came over and held the ice bag steady on my head. Little Belli brought Brown-Bear over and they sang me a song.

Lemon tea for Rainie Marie
'Cause Rainie Marie loves lemon tea.

Kenneth came over and poured the tea into the teacup. He handed it to me and said, "Be careful that your cup doesn't runneth over, Rainie." He giggled.

Great-Gran sat down on the couch and coughed. Then she put her legs up and lay back against the cushions. "Those children wore me out, just listening to them through closed doors."

She shut her eyes and breathed deeply. She looked awfully pale. Before I could ask her if she felt all right, she asked me, "How much you make for all that, Rain?"

"Money, you mean?" I asked.

"Money, I mean."

And then I realized, Mrs. Shanty Sacs had run off without paying me a single penny!

"Not a penny, Great-Gran," I said.

"My Lord in heavenly days, save me," she said.

"Amen," said I.

Great-Gran fell asleep on the couch. Samuel fell asleep on his pile of collage stuff. Kenneth nodded off into his Bible. Louise and Little Belli fell asleep in a heap with Kit, Kat, and Cynthia, and Baby Eddie slurped and burped and snored in his playpen.

I sighed, close to sleep myself. A thought jerked me awake and my eyes flew wide open. I had told Mama I'd get a job and help out with money problems. Today I had a job, but I blew it. What if I could never hold a job? What if I was a complete idiot? What if there was something wrong with me, and everybody knew it, but nobody wanted to hurt my feelings by telling me? What if . . . ?

No way! A person could wear herself down if she let bad thoughts beat her up. Bad thoughts were like hard rain on a hillside garden, washing away all the good soil, all the seeds, all the gardener's hard work. I would not let that happen to me. I had doubted myself once today, when I tried to run away from the angels. I would not doubt myself again. I would be strong.

Mrs. Shanty Sacs and her angels were not the type of family a person would come across every day. Maybe I lost one battle with them, but that didn't mean I'd lose the war, letting my family be split up. As Great-Gran said, "One battle does not a whole war make."

Not even the thought of Aunt Awful babying Mama, making her choose between Brussels sprouts and succotash, was going to get me down. Aunt Awful, thinking everybody should think her way. Aunt Awful, blowing my family up into smithereens. Not even that was going to get me down!

Tomorrow morning, I promised myself, tomorrow morning I would call Mama and tell her it was time for us to come home. Before it was too late.

CHAPTER
ELEVEN

Busy. Busy. Busy. Who was Mama talking to? Or was it old Aunt Awful tying up the phone line?

In the meantime, I fed the little ones the last of the orange juice, and English muffins with butter and sugar. Then I cleaned the breakfast dishes.

"Where's Great-Gran?" I asked Samuel.

"She was here a while ago," he said.

Great-Gran had disappeared again. She had a magical talent, Great-Gran did. Her specialty was the disappearing trick. She did it every day.

"Great-Gran! Great-Gran!" I called as I wandered through the house.

No answer.

I walked over to Kenneth's Bible chair.

"Don't ask me, Rainie Marie," he said, before

I even had a chance to say anything.

"Don't ask you what?" I demanded. I hated it when he thought he could read my mind.

"Where Great-Gran is," he said.

My mind had been read.

"Well, where does she disappear to every day?" I asked. "First my acorn disappears, then Great-Gran. By the way—"

Kenneth interrupted me. "Nope."

"Nope, what?"

"Nope, I haven't seen your acorn, either," he said, and poked his nose back into the story of Job.

I thought, Job and me, we've got a lot in common. I also thought, If I had my acorn, my magic powers would be back. The Mistress of Magic would conjure up Great-Gran easy as anything.

I walked out to the kitchen and opened the cellar door.

The sweet, flowery smell of Great-Gran's air freshener wafted up the cellar steps and into my nose. I heard Great-Gran's hacking cough and finally saw her. She came into the dim light at the foot of the cellar steps. Coughing and wheezing and clinging onto the banister with her left hand, she climbed slowly up. In her right hand, she clutched her special belonging, the box that Samuel had collaged for her.

"Great-Gran, where have you been?" I demanded, standing on the top step, my hands on my hips.

Great-Gran jumped a foot into the air. Her right hand went to her heart. She forgot she had the box in her hand, and she clumped her chest with it pretty hard.

"*Oomph!* My Lord in heavenly days, Great-Granddaughter, you scared me half to death," she scolded me.

She climbed and coughed one more time. I stood back and let her through the door.

"You're coughing a lot," I said.

"Cold. I just got a cold," she explained.

"But you're not sniffling," I pointed out.

"Are you testing me, Great-Granddaughter?" Great-Gran asked peevishly.

"No, ma'am."

"Now, give me some room. I got work to be done." Great-Gran must have gotten her wind back, because she hustled into her room and shut the door with a solid *thunk*.

I called Mama's again, to tell her about Great-

Gran's cough and her disappearing acts every day.

Finally, no busy signal.

Aunt Castina answered. "Rainie Marie, what did you do to Mrs. Shanty Sacs's angels?" she demanded, as soon as she heard my voice.

"The question is, What did Mrs. Shanty Sacs's angels do to me?" I snapped back. My patience was at the end of its rope.

"Don't you go mouthing off to me, little girl. Shanty Sacs called me this very morning and had me on the phone for Lord knows how long! Her angels said you did nothing all day but make them stand in a corner! Mrs. Sacs called you unfit! Now you don't have a job. What are you going to do with your time before you leave Great-Gran's?"

"Oh, nothing. Except maybe take care of all my brothers and sisters. And cook. And clean. And help Louise with her times tables. And help Samuel with his spelling. And shovel all that snow outside. Isn't that enough for me to do before I leave . . . hey, wait a minute! Before I leave Great-Gran's? You mean, we're going home soon? When? Today? Tomorrow?"

"Calm down, now. You know your mama's in no condition to cope. I meant before you leave . . .

er . . . before your trip down to . . . er . . . "

"We're not going anywhere else, are we?" I whispered, afraid she'd hear the question and answer it. But it was a question that had to be answered.

"Nothing is definite, Rain. But I have suggested, I have strongly recommended to your mama, that perhaps your daddy should care for you."

"No!"

"Of course, he'd never be able to handle all of you . . . "

"Right," I agreed with her. "Never in a million years. So we should forget about Tennessee, right?"

Aunt Awful hissed, "So maybe only you and Samuel will go to Tennessee. And the others will go—well—elsewhere."

"Put Mama on the phone!"

"Don't take that tone, miss. I told your mama, I said, 'That daughter of yours will never go for this, but you've got to be strong, for your own sake.' You listen to me, Rainie Marie, your mama is vulnerable at this time. And I consider her my charge, and she will do as I—"

"Put Mama on the phone!" I shrieked.

I heard the receiver on Aunt Castina's end slam down. I pictured it lying on the little table under the phone, its twisted cord dangling off the tabletop. I heard her voice boom out, "Your oldest is on the phone. With one big attitude."

"Hello, Rainie?"

"Mama, we can't go to Tennessee to live!"

"But Castina says—"

"Mama, stop listening to what she says," I yelled.

"But she's always right, dear. Castina has logic; she thinks things out. She has never led me wrong."

"You've got to listen to me, Mama!"

"Rain, I've got to listen to a person who has experience. I've got to listen to a person I can depend on. Don't forget, Castina is an adult. You are only a—"

"I know. Aunt Castina is an adult. I'm only a kid. But, Mama, Aunt Castina is only an aunt, and I'm your daughter. And so are Louise and Little Belli your daughters. And Kenneth and Samuel and Baby Eddie are your sons. And we're your family. And we miss you!"

"You do?" Mama actually sounded surprised. "I

119

hadn't thought of that. I actually hadn't thought of that, Rain."

"Yes, of course we miss you! Families should not be torn asunder," I said, remembering one of Kenneth's favorite lines from the back of his prayer book.

"Well, do you think we could manage somehow?" Mama was wavering. She said, "But I thought you were all happy down there."

"We are happy, visiting here. But we belong home. Home is supposed to be where you're always allowed to go. You say I'm old enough to care for the little ones. You say, 'What would I do without my Rainie Marie?' Mama, we go traveling and traveling, but we're always just waiting to come home. My whole life has been either getting ready for a travel, or being on a travel, wishing I wasn't. We need home, Mama. We need you! I'll get a job. Samuel will get a job! We'll find a place to live. We'll make out," I said.

Mama was quiet. I thought, She's finally listening to me. Making progress, making progress, I thought to myself.

"I'll discuss it with Aunt Castina," Mama said.

"No!"

"No?"

"No!" I yelled, stamping my foot hard into the floor. "Make up your own mind, Mama. Do what I say!" I realized as soon as I said, "Do what I say!" that I'd said too much.

"How is doing what you say making up my own mind? Hold on, your aunt wants to talk to you."

"Rainie Marie?" Aunt Castina's words were so honey sweet, they oozed over the phone line and out of the receiver. "You want what's best for your little mama, don't you?"

"But—"

"And your mama wants what's best for all of you. Don't you, honey?" I heard Aunt Awful ask my mother. Then she started talking to me again. "Your mama's gone to fix us some tea. Listen, Rainie Marie, you're used to bossing your mama around. You can be very domineering, my dear. Well, now is not the time for her to be bamboozled by youngsters. She needs time. You need to give her that time. And I'm here to make sure you do! Ah, a nice cup of tea. Thank you, dear," Aunt Awful had once again turned to my mama. Then Castina's voice, turned back to me, changed, as she changed the subject on me completely. "How's the weather there in Beacon, dear?" she asked, her voice firm and final.

If this conversation had been a football game, Aunt Awful had just grabbed the ball out of my arms and run with it. Touchdown for her side.

When I hung up the phone, I realized I never got a chance to talk to Mama about Great-Gran's cough.

After supper that night, we gathered around in the living room. The little ones wanted me to sing.

"Sure," I said. "Go see if Great-Gran wants to sing, too."

"Can't find her," said Little Belli.

"Rainie Marie to the rescue," I said to her, smiling and getting up.

I went to Great-Gran's bedroom and knocked on the door. It opened immediately, and I looked past Great-Gran into her room. The flowery smell of freshly sprayed air freshener crept into my nose, as it usually did whenever I found Great-Gran behind a closed door. She must love freshly sprayed rooms. A cold breeze gave me goose bumps.

"Great-Gran, why is your window open?"

"Fresh air, girl," Great-Gran said.

"But why fresh air and air freshener, both?" I wanted to know. Was I missing out on a general rule or something, that maybe sprayed air freshener was only safe if you used it with open windows? I remembered hearing somewhere that air freshener didn't just put a good smell into the air. It actually had little things in it that numbed the nerves in your nose so you couldn't smell the bad things. Maybe air freshener gave you cancer, like cigarettes. And you had to mix it with outside air. These are things nobody ever tells a kid.

Great-Gran snapped at me, "Questions, questions! What do you want, anyway?"

I decided to let the air freshener question ride for a while, so I asked instead, "You want to sing?"

"Now that's a question I like," smiled Great-Gran.

We gathered in the living room with Great-Gran's famous hot chocolate recipe. We each had a whole marshmallow floating in it. Louise and Little Belli sat on the floor at my feet. Kenneth lounged under a window, teasing the cats. Samuel sat on our folded-up sofa bed, alongside

Great-Gran, who swung her foot to the beat of
my made-up song.

> *Hope is for the angels,*
> *Hope is for the dogs and cats,*
> *Hope is for the birds and bees*
> *And everything like that.*
> *Hope is for family and home,*
> *Hope is for us, too.*
> *When I find my old acorn*
> *I'll hope for apples and popcorn*
> *And all our troubles to be airborne*
> *Away, away, away.*
> *And we will all go home,*
> *Never more to roam.*
> *And we will all go home.*

As we sat in the golden glow of Great-Gran's
warm winter living room, I thought of Mama
and home. Just as the mug of hot chocolate
warmed my fingers, and the hot chocolate
trickled down my throat and warmed my belly,
the thought of home warmed my heart.

And, once more, my eyes scanned the floor
and all the nooks and the crannies in the room
for that old acorn of mine. For hope.

CHAPTER
TWELVE

There were some things I was not allowed to do at Great-Gran's. She insisted that it was her job to keep us safe as beans. In Great-Gran's eyes, one of the things that would not keep me "safe as beans" was doing the laundry.

"That laundry's way down those dark cellar stairs. It's way down that dark old hallway. I got to keep you safe as beans, Rain. That means the laundry's my job," Great-Gran said.

"But Mama made me promise to help you. And there's so much extra laundry because of us," I argued.

"Never you mind, Rainie Marie."

"But I promised Mama!"

Great-Gran got all deep-eyed. She lowered

her voice and said slowly, "No telling, in this house, what's lurking in those cellar walls."

Maybe Great-Gran was right. I said, "Then I'll make supper tonight. OK?"

"You can do the dishes, too," she said. She is some bargain maker, Great-Gran Gardenia is.

As I chopped tomatoes and celery for that night's casserole, I rubbed the cats' furry backs with my toes. I sang this song to my brothers and sisters, who were clustered under my oak garden, looking at the pictures in Great-Gran's magazines.

I like onions and you like peas,
Celery tastes good with chocolate and cheese,
Only eat spinach soaked in beer,
We're all in the same stew, together here.

The little ones danced around the kitchen floor, tripping over Kit, Kat, and Cynthia.

Suddenly, a deep raspy sound rumbled up the cellar steps. I opened the cellar door an inch.

"Great-Gran?" I called.

From far below, through the dark hole of the cellar, came the sound: Great-Gran's cough.

"*Sh-h-h!*" I quieted the others, and called

again, "Great-Gran?"

No answer.

I said, "I'm going down there."

Louise said, "You're not supposed to. It's haunted!"

I heard the heavy rumbling sound again. "Samuel, keep your eye on the little ones. I'm going down."

Kenneth sprang up. "Cellar's got spiders and rats, Rainie Marie! And . . . other things."

I gave them all the eye that meant I meant business, and started down.

As I got to the second step, I heard the cellar door creak shut behind me. I spun around and tried the knob, pushing against the old wood of the door. It would not budge!

The steps were dimly lit by a lone dangling lightbulb that shone weakly at the bottom of the stairs. I put my hand along the shadowed wall. It was cold and slimy.

Holding my breath, I took one step and then another. And then another, down, down, down. I could imagine the ghosts of those that had died here, watching me.

Something brushed against my cheek! I yelped and put my hand up. A cobweb. Cobwebs meant spiders. Fat, black, hairy spiders filled with green pus and poison. Crawly things that were silent as the fog that rolls in. Crawly things that climbed up your clothes and pounced onto your face before you even knew it! Every bone in my body turned to Jell-O.

When I reached the bottom, the lightbulb cast my shadow against the cement wall. I turned to face the narrow hallway that ran under Great-Gran's house. Way down, a pale light shone through an open doorway, and I heard the quiet mumble of the dryer spinning clothes. That was where my great-grandmother was. In the laundry room.

I held my breath, not wanting to awaken the dead from the cellar walls. I tried to move but couldn't. Then, the rumble of that awful cough racked its way through the dank cellar air.

"Great-Gran?" My voice was hardly as loud as the scratch of a spider's legs. "Great-Gran?" I called again, forcing my voice to be louder.

"Rainie Marie?" A weak sigh with my name on it floated out on the light through the doorway.

No time for fear! I told myself. I ran down the hall and slid into the light. A funny, foul smell hit me in the face.

Cigarette smoke!

There was Great-Gran, crouched on the floor by the washer, a burning cigarette in her hand. She clutched her chest, coughing.

"Rainie, seems I got a little trouble," she rasped.

"C'mon. I'll help you upstairs," I said.

"Don't really think I can move at the moment," she murmured.

"But you can't stay down here," I said.

"Think maybe you better get me some help," Great-Gran said, falling into another coughing fit.

I yanked the cigarette out from between her fingers, crushed it on the cement floor, and kicked it into the shadows. I took a warm, folded towel from the pile on the dryer and covered her thin, shaking shoulders. I took another and covered her knees.

"Great-Gran, I'm going to call an ambulance. Samuel and Kenneth will be right down. Don't worry. I'm taking care of everything. Everything will be fine," I promised her, already on my way.

Out of the corner of my eye, I spotted my great-grandma's dream box. It sat half-hidden on the shelf behind the washer. Its lid yawned open like a great mouth. Lined up inside, like white sardines, were cigarettes! The cigarettes that had given Great-Stepdaddy cancer! No wonder

Great-Gran kept disappearing. No wonder she always used air freshener and had open windows even in the dead of winter. We, the proud non-smoking family, would have discovered her secret!

I ran down the hall, up the stairs, and rammed my shoulder into the door. It lurched open.

"Samuel! Kenneth! Get to the laundry room!" I yelled.

I ran to the phone, scanned Great-Gran's emergency number list, and dialed the ambulance. I screamed to them what had happened and gave our address. I slammed down the phone and turned to my brothers and sisters.

This is what I did:

I tightened Baby Eddie's safety belt so he wouldn't slip out of his high chair. I gave him his milk cup and Kit's rubber ball to roll on the high-chair tray.

I said to the little ones at the kitchen table, "Stay!"

I shoved crackers and jelly and a spoon at them, ordering them, "Eat!"

I said quick prayers to God and to every saint I could think of.

And I thanked my lucky stars that I worked well under pressure. The Mistress of Magic had not entirely disappeared.

CHAPTER
THIRTEEN

Some things in our lives don't seem real. Like scary things, like when someone you really love is very sick. And when you're waiting for help to come, and it seems that days and weeks and years pass before the help comes, even though it is really only minutes that have passed.

Some things in our lives seem not real. They feel like a dream, they look like a dream, they even sound like a dream—that hearing-through-water kind of sound that dreams often have.

I know it is real that the ambulance got to Great-Gran's on Oldhome Road in ten minutes, but it seemed like forever before I saw the flashing, brilliant white and red lights jet-stream up the street and heard the siren slice the air.

I know the rescue people jumped out of the ambulance and scurried up the walk, carrying equipment for Great-Gran. But they seemed to be slogging through molasses and mud.

It wasn't until they clattered down the cellar stairs like giant beetles that time righted itself and sped up to normal.

I sat with my brothers and sisters around the kitchen table. Baby Eddie sat at my side, in his high chair. We listened closely to what was going on in the cellar.

The cellar door was open, and we could hear the voices of the rescue people, but we couldn't hear the words. Louise sniffled twice, sneezed a huge, juicy sneeze all over her untouched crackers and peanut butter, and burst into tears.

Little Belli did the same, except she didn't sneeze.

Samuel *tsked* and *humphed* and hunched his shoulders and squeezed his eyes tight shut and sniffed. He wiped his nose on his hand, then swung around in his seat, so we saw only his back. His shoulders shook in little shivers.

Baby Eddie played with the crackers on his high-chair tray and hummed a tuneless tune.

Kenneth bent his head and prayed.

I did the same. I prayed a prayer Mama had taught me. The Sisters of the Sacred Heart had taught Mama this prayer when she was in the sixth grade, just like me.

> O most Sacred Heart of Jesus,
> I have asked you for many favors,
> but I plead for this one.

Then you were supposed to name your favor, and then you were supposed to say a Hail Mary, an Our Father, and a Glory Be.

"This prayer is for only the most ultimate, important favors, not just any old thing," Mama had warned me.

Saving Great-Gran's life definitely qualified as a most ultimate, important thing. So I used the prayer. But I forgot how to say half of the Hail Mary and I only remembered two words from the Glory Be, which were glory and be. So I just said the "O most Sacred Heart" part and the Our Father over and over and over again.

Finally they brought Great-Gran up on the stretcher. Her face was pale. Her eyes were closed. She was no longer coughing. She seemed barely able to breathe.

One of the rescue people, whose name tag said GRACE, came over to the table while the others were carrying Great-Gran out through the living room and the front door on the stretcher.

The rescue person named Grace said to me, "Now, do you have someone to care for you youngsters?"

"Of course," I said, starting to explain that I was in charge.

Grace interrupted me. "Good. Call 'em and get 'em over here. Can't stay by yourselves, y'know. Bye!"

And she was gone with the others, in the blare of the siren.

Who was I going to call? Mrs. Shanty Sacs? Who *should* I call? I didn't know anybody in Beacon. Oh, well—I could take care of things myself, just like always. Although it would have been much easier with my acorn. The Mistress of Magic would have no problem with a situation like this. But even without my acorn, I could handle things. Call for help? I didn't think so!

The one person I did call was Mama.

"Keep your eye on Baby Eddie, Samuel," I ordered.

"OK." Samuel slumped in his chair, folding paper napkins into shapes of stars and moons.

Little Belli was sound asleep, her head on the table in a mess of cracker crumbs and peanut butter mush. Louise was nodding off to the same land of sleep.

Kenneth still prayed, or maybe he was asleep, too. His head was bent down to his chest.

I went to the phone and dialed Mama's number, wondering how I would tell her about Great-Gran.

I decided straight-out was the best way.

Mama did not take the news well.

"Oh no!" she exclaimed. "Haven't I got enough, with Mr. Sugar gone? What's the good Lord trying to do to me?"

"Mama, everything's under control," I said. But comforting over the phone did not work well.

"You tell me that, with your Great-Gran in the hospital? And you stuck down there all by yourself with all those kids? Lord!" Mama shrieked. I could picture her tugging at her hair, the way she did when she was real upset.

"Mama, Great-Gran's in good hands. You once told me the hospital was 'good hands.' Remember? And they said they'd call me soon's Great-Gran's settled. Then I'll call you. And the little ones are fine. They're all asleep with their heads in crackers and peanut butter. You want me to wake them, so you can talk to them?"

She did.

By the time she was done talking, I was busy fixing tuna and noodles for supper. It seemed the appetites of the little ones were strong as weeds and not harmed by storm or catastrophe.

Kenneth came over to me and said, "Mama said she'd call back when arrangements were made."

"What arrangements?" I asked. The word *arrangements* scared me, unless I was the one doing the arranging.

Kenneth shrugged and flung himself down on the floor, amid the cats and Louise and Little Belli. The girls were still bleary-eyed from their tabletop nap and sniffly from the whole day.

I trailed after Kenneth and asked, "Did Mama mention anything about Aunt Castina?"

Kenneth shook his head no.

"Did Mama mention anything about Tennessee?"

Kenneth shrugged.

"Well, did she or didn't she?" I kept after him.

"Well, Aunt Castina was talking in the background. I think maybe she said 'Tennessee.' Or maybe she was just talking about somebody's tennis knee. Do you think, Rainie Marie?" he asked with desperation in his voice. Kenneth did not want another travel, any more than Samuel or I did.

"Tennis knee. Yeah, right," I sneered at him.

Louise's head snapped up at the word "Tennessee." She burst into tears for the second time that day. Louise was on a roll. And judging from past crying rolls in Louise's life, this was just the beginning.

Louise cried, "See, Rainie Marie, see? I'm never gonna see you again. You're," sniff, sob, "going," sob, cough, "to," hic, "*Tennessee!* And

I'm going," sob, "*Elsewhere!*"

"Wait a minute. How do you know you're going elsewhere?" I asked, remembering the phone conversation I had had with Mama and Aunt Castina, and remembering that I had not told Louise about it.

"I know how to listen on an extension," said Louise, tears forgotten for the moment and nose snootily stuck in the air.

All the sobbing and carrying-on was too much for Little Belli to listen to. She cried right along with Louise. They both woke up Baby Eddie, who had still been napping in his high chair. Then he decided to join the chorus. Oh, brother, this was all I needed. This was definitely the most waterlogged winter recess I'd ever had.

There're some people on this earth who push help away. Mama was one of them. She had us, but when trouble came, she didn't know what to do with us. She did not know how to use the comfort we offered her.

She only knew how to listen to her big sister, Boss of the Universe, Castina.

Cleaning up the tuna and noodle dishes

after supper, I said to myself, "If I'm so good at making arrangements and decisions, if I'm so good at organizing and taking charge, why do I let myself get pushed around so much? Maybe it's time for me to start making decisions for this family.

"If only I had my acorn," I said to the sink full of suds. "Then I'd know what to do.

"Mama," I whispered to myself, "you need me and you don't know it. The more shoulders you have to lean on, the lighter your trouble will be. Why can't you see that?"

But Mama would not hear my whispers tonight. And the way things were going, I doubted if God could hear my prayers! Standing amid the worried babble of the little ones, I felt utterly alone.

"Stupid acorn!" I yelled at the soapsuds. And with a mean swish of the dishcloth, I sent those soapsuds flying all over the counter.

CHAPTER
FOURTEEN

That evening, we waited for the hospital to call with news of Great-Gran Gardenia. We sat in Great-Gran's cozy living room, but it didn't seem cozy anymore. It was as if the light had changed from warm yellow to cold blue, from safe to scary. It was the same living room, but not the same. Like the difference between Great-Gran's famous hot chocolate recipe and Aunt Castina's hot carob no-sugar-no-fat-no-taste recipe. They were both hot cocoa, but definitely different.

"I wish this living room felt like it did before Great-Gran got sick," said Samuel out of the clear blue sky.

"That's exactly what I was thinking.

Exactly!" I exclaimed. Samuel and I truly lived along the same path. He was always surprising me by saying just what I was thinking.

We sat in silence and looked at each other and listened to the songs of Great-Gran's old house. It was singing sad songs tonight. The click of the old clock on the wall ticked the time away.

The jangle of the telephone made us all jump.

On my way to answer the phone, I plunged my hand deep into my pocket, hoping for a miracle.

No miracle; no acorn.

If I had had my acorn in my hand, answering the phone would have been easier.

"Is this the residence of Mrs. Gardenia Flowers?" the voice at the other end asked.

I gulped. The voice sounded official.

"Yes," I answered, choking over the simple word.

"And is this Rainie Marie Greene?" the voice at the other end continued.

"Yes," I choked again.

"Ah, Miss Greene, this is Dr. Muldune. I'm

happy to tell you that your great-grandmother is doing fine."

In my brain, a chorus burst out, singing hallelujahs. The doctor talked on, but I barely listened to what he said. My heart and my head were full of rejoicing.

I ran into the living room after I had hung up, shouting, "She's going to be OK! She's going to be OK!"

The others applauded and cheered.

"This calls for a toast," declared Kenneth, getting up from his Bible chair.

"Toast! Toast with butter!" cried Little Belli, ready to celebrate through her stomach once again.

"Not that kind of toast, pie-face!" laughed Samuel, giving her a nudge and following Kenneth out to the kitchen.

They returned in a few minutes with a tray of paper cups and a carton of milk.

"Why do we hafta have milk? Why can't we have juice? Or soda!" complained Louise.

Samuel answered her matter-of-factly, "'Cause we're out of juice and soda. That's why."

I dragged in Baby Eddie's high chair and

buckled him in. I helped Kenneth pour the milk and pass out the cups.

"A toast," said Kenneth grandly, holding his cup to the ceiling.

"A toast to Great-Gran!" added Samuel, holding his cup up also.

"Toast!" we all cried, holding our cups up, the way we'd seen grown-ups do on TV.

"Toat!" yelled Baby Eddie. Baby Eddie rarely spoke at all. We stopped in our tracks and looked at him. Proudly, he raised his cup up high over his head. Then he tipped it and poured his milk all over his head.

"Yuck!" said Louise and Little Belli.

Baby Eddie felt the milk pouring down his face and neck, onto his shirt. He screamed like a demon.

"Tell him about crying over spilt milk, Rain," advised Kenneth, laughing into his cup.

I ignored the whole thing, the mature way. I snapped at the others, "Do you want to hear what the doctor said about Great-Gran, or don't you?"

I told them what the doctor had told me. "Great-Gran didn't have a heart attack," I said.

A sigh of relief circled the living room. I hoisted Baby Eddie out of his high chair and dried his head with the hem of my shirt. I jiggled him on my knee. He banged his hand against his milk cup, humming contentedly.

I continued, "What she had was like a warning."

Kenneth said, "God gives warnings to his children."

"Shut up, Kenneth!" said Samuel. "Go on, Rainie Marie."

Louise started to tell Samuel not to say shut up, but thought better of it. "Go on, Rainie Marie," she said.

"Thank you both," I said sarcastically. Hopefully, they'd be quiet until I was finished. I had to word this carefully, for Great-Gran's sake.

"Anyway, Great-Gran's heart had a heart aryth . . . arya . . . amith . . . oh, some big word! Anyway, she's got a pill for it now, and one for her blood pressure. She has to eat food with no fat and no salt."

"Jack Sprat! Eat! No! Fat!" burst Little Belli.

I carried on, pretending that these outbursts just didn't happen. The mature way. "And she has to take a walk every day. And she has to make certain other . . . uh . . . adjustments," I said.

I had to protect Great-Gran's dark secret. It wasn't right to tell about the cigarettes. Mama had taught us how terrible and disgusting smoking was, and how stupid smokers were. If the little ones found out Great-Gran was a smoker, they would be confused. And that would not help Mama *or* Great-Gran. And I had to help them both through this period of sadness and sickness. Some things are best left outside with the fertilizer, as Great-Gran loved to say.

Little Belli asked, "What's dejusmins?"

Samuel said, "Adjustments. It means, take the bumpy road of life sometimes, but then get back on the smooth road."

"Huh?" asked Little Belli.

"Huh?" I asked, too. Samuel was not so hot at definitions.

I said, "It just means change. Like what we do every time we go on a travel. We do an adjustment. We do a change."

"Like diapers?" asked Little Belli.

"Huh?" I asked once again.

"Like change diapers. Dejusmins diapers," Little Belli explained.

"Oh. Um," I started.

Louise perked up. She said, oh-so-cutely, "Oh, Rainie Marie, from the sweet smell of Baby Eddie, I think he needs an adjustment right now!"

Oh, brother.

And then Louise said, "When's Great-Gran coming home, anyway? We need juice and soda."

"Louise, I can always count on you to think of your own selfish self in times like this," I said.

Samuel pushed his breath out through his teeth and shook his head at Louise, showing his disapproval. Kenneth sucked his teeth, and Little Belli stuck her tongue out at Louise. Baby Eddie, not understanding what was going on but wanting to join in, slipped off my lap, waddled over to Louise, and banged on her knee with his hands, a two-fisted attack.

"Cut that out, booger machine!" yelled Louise. She jumped up and flounced out of the room.

The phone rang again. Saved by the bell!

"Hello?" I said into the phone.

"Rain, it's Mama. Aunt Castina said she's coming to stay with Great-Gran. She already talked to the hospital and to your great-grandma."

"Yes, ma'am." If Aunt Castina were here, Samuel and I wouldn't be sent to Tennessee. The others wouldn't be sent to Elsewhere. We could go home! Or if I couldn't convince Mama she needed us, then we could stay here for a while. I could help Great-Gran get better and quit smoking.

"Rain?"

"Yes, Mama?"

"I, well, you . . . well, maybe you shouldn't stay in Beacon. You think it'd be too much for Castina? You know, since she's not used to kids?" Mama's voice sounded small as a ladybug.

"Mama, you're right! We shouldn't stay here. We'll come home! Tomorrow!" My heart burst with blossoms of daffodils and tulips in my chest.

"Um, that's not what I meant. Aunt Castina says you'd be better off, uh, um, down . . . um . . . well, with your daddy."

The daffodils and tulips withered and died. My heart sank to my knees.

Mama talked on, of how she missed us so, of how the bills were piling up and she had to face them all alone. She said if Aunt Castina hadn't been there, she wouldn't know what to do. She talked of how Mr. Sugar's ghost came to her in the middle of each night and told her to take care of herself.

"He says, 'Little lady, you take care of yourself, and the others will follow suit,'" Mama said.

My heart sank even below my knees, to the floor. I looked at the floor, seeing if my heart was visible against the wood.

I caught sight of a tiny shiny thing under the telephone table. It was a thing that glimmered in the shadow. As Mama kept talking softly, I got on my knees and bent over to look into the dusty darkness under the table. Mama's voice became a dim hum against my ear.

Because there, in the dark, was a diamond shining through a caramel.

My acorn!

I gently covered it with my fingers and drew it to me. So careful, so careful—was it a dream, this acorn?

I held it in my hand. Power surged into me,

through my skin, through my hand, up my arm, through my veins. The power of magic!

My acorn! The Mistress of Magic was back!

I spoke, clearly and strongly, into the phone.

"Mama, listen to me. I am not going to travel again! We are a family, not a Gypsy caravan! Not migrating ducks! We need to stay together!"

Mama sighed. "Maybe you better talk with your aunt, Rain."

"I will, Mama, I will talk with her! And I will tell Aunt Awful just what I think of her!"

I told Mama I loved her and hung up the phone. I held my precious belonging in my open palm. The light danced around its smooth brown skin and shot off into the dim hallway.

Victory was mine! Home was mine!

Aunt Awful was mine!

And with that thought, my acorn broke into two parts, sad and unshiny, in my hand. It cracked along a line of tooth marks from Kit, Kat, and Cynthia. Its crown fell one way; its round body rolled the other.

"But you're still my acorn, aren't you?" I

asked, fitting the parts back together, willing them to stick.

My life was a series of omens. And I made a choice to go with the good ones and fight the bad.

CHAPTER
FIFTEEN

Y ou're going to tell Aunt Awful what you think of her?" remarked Kenneth.

"You think you're going to convince Aunt Awful that she is wrong and you are right? Oh, boy, Rainy-day Rainie Marie. Are you stupid or crazy or what!?" exclaimed Samuel.

"Stupid *and* crazy *and* or-what!" answered smart-mouth Louise.

Maybe they were right. Maybe I would never be able to face Aunt Awful. What could I have been thinking? The Mistress of Magic? Oh, brother, just what I need. A delusion. My acorn was broken. I failed at taking care of that, I failed at taking care of Mrs. Shanty Sacs's brats, I failed at taking care of Great-Gran. How could

I think I could take care of Aunt Awful? I must be stupid. I must be crazy. *And* or-what. My decision the other night, to not let self-doubt get to me? Yeah. Right.

As I tucked the little ones into their beds that night, Little Belli asked, "Will you sing to us, Rainie Marie?"

"Yeah, Rain. Sing. Sing a happy song," demanded Louise. She had told me, after I hung up from Mama's phone call, that she had been listening on the extension.

"When are you going to ever learn?" I asked her, angry that she had been eavesdropping again.

"I think I did . . . when I overheard Mama say you had to be moved to Tennessee again," Louise had said in a sad voice.

"So now you want a happy song?" I asked Louise, tightening her fluffy white blanket around her.

"I think I need it," she answered in a sleep-blurry voice.

I went from bedroom to bedroom, turning out lights and kissing the brothers and sisters on their soapy-smelling, freshly scrubbed foreheads.

I sang, as I visited each sleepyhead:

Clumps of daisies in the garden,
Sets of dishes on the shelves,
Bundles of books in the bookcase,
But we're to be ourselves.
If stars have constellations,
And suns have families of stars,
And clouds float in families of cotton,
Where is our family, where is ours?

I sang them the only song that could come from my heart tonight.

Little Belli hid her head, along with Brown-Bear's head, under the covers.

"Bummer," said Louise.

Samuel agreed, calling from the living-room sofa bed, "Yeah, bummer."

In his room, Kenneth tucked his Bible under his pillow and buried his head deeply into the pillow, as if he wanted to press right into his Good Book.

"Rainy-day Rainie Marie," he grumbled.

And even Baby Eddie cooed from his nest in his playpen, *"Bum bum bum bum!"*

All the lights were turned out; I wandered

into the kitchen, turned on the amber-colored light over the sink, and put the kettle on for a cup of cocoa. I pulled Great-Gran's stool up to the kitchen counter. When the kettle whistled for me, I poured the steaming water into a mug of cocoa powder and sugar.

"I think I'll skip the marshmallow," I muttered to myself, not feeling in a festive mood. Some things are better enjoyed with the right people. As far as marshmallows went, Great-Gran was the right people.

I perched on the stool and put my elbows on the counter, holding my face over the steaming mug. The steam felt good.

The house was as silent as the banks of starlit snow outside. Once in a while, the old floorboards groaned, or the paint-chipped windowsills moaned lightly, singing a lonesome song. In this house where the ghosts walked, I was in charge. I was in charge of keeping us together. I was in charge of talking to Aunt Awful, who would be here tomorrow.

Mama had said on the phone, "Do you want Castina to come down to Beacon tonight?"

"No!" I answered, very quickly.

"You sure, Rain?"

"Yes, ma'am. We're all fine here. Safe as beans."

But were we?

My very next thought was, "Ouch." Because I woke up to sunlight streaming in through the kitchen window, shining on the counter where I was bent over. I had slept on the stool, drooped over the counter, all night.

Later, after breakfast, Aunt Awful swept in, in a flurry of snow and cloak.

"Well, my favorite nieces and nephews," she said, looking us over the way a pirate looks at stolen treasure. "Are you all ready?"

"Ready for what?" I asked.

"Well, for your next exciting travel," she chirped, a cheery vulture.

"I think maybe we better go sit down," suggested Samuel, in a rare moment of thoughtfulness for others.

We went into Great-Gran's living room. Aunt Awful asked, "Who would like some of my wonderful hot chocolate?"

"No, thank you," we mumbled together.

This was one of the few things we all agreed on.

"Well, then. Let's talk. Your Mama and I stayed up half the night discussing your . . . um . . . future. We were on the phone the other half of the night!" She giggled nervously. I looked closely at her. In my mind, I was picturing her sitting there in Great-Gran's favorite chair, foaming and drooling at the mouth, rubbing her hands together, her nails foot-long claws. I pictured her with fangs six inches long, waiting to sink into us and tear us apart. But she sat there, only Aunt Castina, surveying us.

"I should call Mama," I said, starting to get up.

Castina help up a hand in a stop signal. "No need," she said. "Everything's set." She sighed deeply, settled back comfortably in Great-Gran's chair, crossed her legs, and continued. "I know you all think I'm terrible, that I'm trying to break up your family. Really I'm not. But since I was seventeen, I've been in charge of your mama."

She paused, then went on, "Your mother is lucky that she has sisters who care and are willing to lend a helping hand. Your aunt Pludy has taken you in several times before. Your aunt Cassandra in Mahwah would love to have you. One or two of you, at least. You are lucky that you have a daddy who loves you. I have arranged things to be the best for your mama. And for you."

"But you don't know what's best for us," I said. "And you have no right to arrange things for us. You are not boss of us. We have our own minds and should make our own decisions."

"Young lady, you listen to me," said Aunt Castina.

"No. It's your turn to listen to me," I was finally standing up to Aunt Awful. "It is always you telling Mama, you telling Mama, like you were Boss of the Universe. You're not thinking of us. You're thinking of your own self and what you want. And you want just you and Mama, together. Well, Mama has children, and we are going to stick together, through sickness and health, for richer and poorer!"

"This is not a wedding ceremony," Aunt Awful cut in, in her sneery voice. "And arrangements have been made."

"But—"

"And that is that. Now, Rainie Marie, you will be taking Samuel to your daddy's, in Tennessee. Kenneth, you will be living with your aunt Pludy in Poughkeepsie. Aren't you the lucky one. You'll get to see your mama lots!" Aunt Awful bent over toward Kenneth, words dripping off her lips like melted butter. Kenneth scrunched way back in his chair, getting as far from her as possible.

As if she hadn't done enough, she continued, "Louise, you and Little Belli will go to Aunt Cassandra's in Mahwah."

"But I never even seen any old Aunt Cassandra in Mahwah. I wouldn't know her if she bit me on the leg!" shouted Louise.

Aunt Awful ignored her. "And I will take Baby Eddie myself. To Newburgh. To a wonderful lady I know through church, who has agreed to take him in."

There were no words to say. We stared at Aunt Awful, the Grim Reaper, the killer of our family.

And still she continued. "Your mama wants what's best for you. She does not want to cast her problems upon her young ones." Aunt

Awful was enunciating. When she was angry or upset, she didn't yell. She enunciated. I knew she was waiting for a barrage of tears and screams and arguments. But she didn't get it. We just sat and stared.

Finally, I said in a whisper, the strongest voice I could muster up, "My family's going to be spread all over the country!"

"Don't be so melodramatic, Rainie Marie," said my aunt. "Someday you'll all be back together." She hesitated and then said, "I'm sure of it."

I had learned that whenever adults said, "I'm sure of it," it means that they're really not sure of anything at all. *Sure* was one of those paper-thin words with nothing behind it to hold it up.

There was no point in wasting my breath talking to Aunt Castina. She had made up her mind and Mama's mind. My family was being spread like daisy seeds by the wind.

Was I strong enough to fight the wind?

CHAPTER
SIXTEEN

Monday morning. Back in Poughkeepsie, winter recess was over. Natasha and our cousins, Aunt Pludy's kids, and all our friends were all going back to school. Soon they'd be doing double-digit multiplication, or trying to figure out how to spell *miraculous*, or underlining the proper nouns in a sentence. Or maybe they'd be singing in music, or drawing in art, or climbing ropes in gym.

But we were in Beacon, and we were packing. Again.

Packing did not take us long. There was not much to pack. And besides, we were used to it.

Great-Gran was scheduled to come home from the hospital Tuesday afternoon. We were to be gone by then.

"But can't we even say good-bye?" asked Louise, still on her tearful roll.

"It's best that your great-grandmother comes home to a peaceful house," said Aunt Awful.

"We have peace," said Little Belli. She was tickling Baby Eddie's feet, and he was cooing. Kit, Kat, and Cynthia were snuggling up, looking for attention since Great-Gran was away. There was peace, in bits and pieces scattered around.

"Peace and quiet," said Aunt Awful, casting a sour eye at us.

Louise started wrapping up her spider plant.

"What are you doing to your great-grandmother's plant?" asked Aunt Awful.

"It's my plant," explained Louise.

"Well, it will do very well in that window. Don't touch it."

"But I have to bring it with me!" Louise's voice rose.

"No!" said Aunt Awful.

"Yes!" replied Louise.

Aunt Awful stormed over to Louise and slapped her hand. "Don't touch!"

Louise slapped Aunt Awful's hand right back

in a split second, before she could think better of it.

Aunt Awful gasped. She turned to me and said, "Rainie Marie, I believe you have purposely turned the young ones against me. Why? Why, Rainie?"

She said to Louise, "I'm so sorry for slapping you. Would you let me talk to your sister alone, dear?" She spoke quietly and politely, as if she meant the apology.

Louise nodded, looking at Aunt Awful with wide, wet eyes. Louise was surprised at Aunt Awful's new gentle tone. She walked through the swinging door, and I heard water run in the kitchen.

Aunt Awful went to the chair her purse sat on. She rummaged around inside, drew something out, and closed her hand around it, making it impossible for me to see what it was. She came back over to me and pulled me down next to her on the couch. We sat side by side.

"I understand you had an acorn, and that you lost it. Is that correct?" she asked me.

"Yes. But I found it," I told her.

"I'm glad. That acorn is important to you, isn't it?" she asked.

I looked at her in wonder. What interest would a person like Aunt Awful have in my acorn? I was surprised she even knew about it. Then she held her closed hand in front of me, opened it up, and showed me what she had taken from her purse.

In the palm of her hand was a small round pink stone. It was dull of color and looked rubbed smooth.

"Do you know what this is, Rain?" asked Aunt Awful.

"A rock. A stone," I answered.

"Nope. It's my piece of magic, my piece of the home and family I grew up in."

I looked at her. My jaw felt as though it had dropped down to my waist, in shock.

My aunt said, "Surprised? Well, I have my little pet quirks. Like you, Rainie Marie. When my mother, your grandmother, got sick, I took over her jobs at home. One was tending her garden. Mother loved flowers."

"Just like Great-Gran," I said.

"Just like Great-Gran," she agreed. "We never had much money, so she didn't go out and buy plants and seeds and things. But friends and neighbors would send along cuttings and slips from their gardens. Mother would transplant them and pay so much attention to them, you'd have thought they were her children. And she could tell you exactly who gave her what plant. She never forgot." Aunt Castina laughed, remembering.

She continued, "When she became ill, I took over the garden. I liked doing it! I was tending not only flowers, but friendships and memories! This stone is from the garden's border. Mom had a gentleman friend. Andrew. Like your mama's Mr. Sugar. He gave her these lovely stones, and she put an edge all around her garden with them. They looked so pretty."

"Did he die?" I asked.

"No, dear. My mother did. And I was left with the girls and the garden. Think of how scared I was, Rainie Marie! Thank the Lord, your great-gran stepped in. She helped me so much with Cassandra, Pludy, and your mama. But the garden was all mine. If I failed and let the garden die, I was letting all those memories die. How could I do that to the memory of my mother?" Aunt Castina actually had tears in her eyes. I didn't think it was possible!

"You were scared, Aunt Castina?" I asked, incredulous.

"Sure was. This stone—I don't know why I chose this one. Maybe because of the color. Or maybe because it fit into the palm of my hand so well. But one day, I picked it up and never again put it down. I considered it my strength, because it was part of my mother's love. I swore to myself I would not let the garden go—that the garden would blossom and bloom. Maybe to other people it seemed silly, but not to me!"

"Did it blossom and bloom?"

"It did, and it still does. Sometime, I'll take you by that house. The people who live there now seemed to sense that it was a special garden. They've cared for it just fine. When you give something your all, Rainie Marie, chances are it will not fail."

"I'll never be able to see it. You're sending me away to Tennessee," I grumbled.

"For your mama's sake," she said.

We sat quietly. My aunt rubbed the stone in her hand. I rubbed the two pieces of my acorn in my pocket.

My aunt whispered, "Your mama's my garden

now, Rain. I love her like she was my own child."

I stared at my aunt, eye to eye. "I love her, too."

"I want her to thrive, like Mother's garden did," said Aunt Castina.

"I have a garden, too, you know. It's my family, and I want them to bloom and blossom. Together!" I said.

We stared at each other, close and long. It seemed there were no words left to say. We each had spoken our mind. And now we each understood the other. I understood Aunt Castina was doing what she thought would be best for our family. I felt that she thought the same of me.

Aunt Castina was zooming around the house, making sure all was set for our next travel. It was early Tuesday morning, and our travel sacks were by the door.

In a light voice and with forced cheerfulness, Aunt Castina asked for the hundredth time, "Now, are you sure you've got everything?"

Little Belli hugged Brown-Bear close to her heart. Samuel's collage bag had a few new lumps in it, from odds and ends that Great-Gran had given him. And Kenneth had his Bible all ready for this new trip.

"Got your tickets?" Aunt Castina asked me.

"Yes'm."

Our aunt floundered through the living room, checking the clock every two minutes.

I wondered if she knew Great-Gran smoked. I wondered if she would be patient at helping Great-Gran quit smoking. I thought that she would be kind. I would not have thought that before we had our talk.

I wondered if Great-Gran would cry when she found us gone without a good-bye.

I held three envelopes. One was large and blue and white. In it were two bus tickets to Tennessee. The second envelope was small and green. It held one bus ticket to Poughkeepsie. The last envelope was medium-size and red. It held two bus tickets to Mahwah, New Jersey.

"What about Baby Eddie's ticket?" I asked. Baby Eddie was sitting on the floor, chewing on his thumbs. I tickled him behind the ears. He loved that, just like Kit, Kat, and Cynthia all loved to be tickled behind the ears. The church lady who was taking Baby Eddie would not do this, I thought.

Aunt Castina said, "Remember? I told you I was taking him myself to Newburgh."

"When?" I asked.

"Right after you all get on your buses. Before your great-grandmother comes home from the hospital. I want to get a taxi early enough, so I won't keep your poor great-grandmother waiting in that hospital lobby. I'll probably have the taxi stop right at the hospital, after I get back from delivering Baby Eddie."

Delivering Baby Eddie? What was he, a pizza? I wondered.

"Why are you taking a taxi? Why aren't you taking your own car?" I asked. Her car was sitting in front of the house, steel gray in the early sun.

"How'm I going to manage first a baby, and then a sickly old woman, and drive at the same time? Really, Rainie Marie, you're slipping!" she said.

My aunt rattled around the house, touching things and rearranging things unnecessarily. Much as she was doing to my family.

We sat lined up on the couch. I had Baby Eddie on my lap. Ducklings on the move again. But this time, our line of ducklings had been exploded into a million different parts.

I put Baby Eddie on Samuel's lap. Kenneth reached over and took him onto his lap. Then Louise and Little Belli took him for themselves. They all wanted to share in their last minutes together.

I walked over to Great-Gran's desk and found her roll of Scotch tape. I took my acorn out of my pocket, held the two pieces together, and taped them together. The pieces no longer looked quite as sad as they once had. And the clear tape added a little shine. I put the acorn back into my pocket, deep and secure, as far as it would go.

Aunt Castina asked for the thousandth time, "You sure you got everything?"

I had felt sad before. Now I felt beyond sad. I was the color of winter rain. I sank back onto the couch among my brothers and sisters. Samuel was beside me. He plunked his collage bag onto my knee.

"Think I'll have time to do a collage for Great-Gran?" he asked.

I looked up at the clock on the wall. Five after seven.

"We don't have to be at the bus station until

nine. I think you'll have time," I said. Samuel got busy, tearing bits of paper and pasting them helter-skelter on a sheet of brown wrapping paper. His fingers worked frantically, but then suddenly stopped. Samuel abandoned working and stared out the window, his thoughts far, far away.

I thought of Poughkeepsie, and my oak tree. When would I ever see them again? I thought of Mad Hattie's Wig and Hat Shop, the Caribbean Foods Store, and Professor Strange's Tea Garden. I thought of my friend Natasha and of the 7-Eleven across the street from my apartment. I thought of Mama sitting in her rocker by the front window, watching the big kids dance in the parking lot to the music from their huge radios.

Kenneth looked down the line of ducklings at us. He nodded and opened his Bible.

"Would you like me to read aloud to you?" he asked.

"That would be nice, Kenneth," I said. Usually we did not like Kenneth to read aloud to us. He always got swept away by his own performance and then expected applause. But the thought of his soft, even voice seemed soothing this morning.

He began:

God will put his angels in charge of you
to protect you wherever you go.
They will hold you up with their hands
to keep you from hurting your feet on the stones.
You will trample down lions and snakes,
fierce lions and poisonous snakes.

When he was done, he closed the Bible and looked out the window. He did not seem to expect applause this time.

Samuel and I both said, "Thank you" to Kenneth, who had told us to trample down lions and snakes, fierce lions and poisonous snakes.

CHAPTER
SEVENTEEN

Louise and Little Belli got up from the couch and sat down at my feet.

Little Belli said, "Sing for us, Rainie Marie."

Lousie said, "Yes. It may be the last song."

Little Belli looked at Louise. Crystal globes formed at the corners of her eyes. Her tears slid down in straight lines, over the roundness of her cheeks.

Baby Eddie was once again in my lap, and I held him tight. My throat felt like it had several balloons in it. I swallowed and said, "OK. Let's have a happy song."

First of all, remember:
You are just a kid,

And because you're just a kid,
You're supposed to act like one!
So when your nose itches, don't scratch it—
Pick it! Pick it! Pick it!
Second of all, remember:
Your mother's diamond earrings
Look best when pasted on
Your ratty Barbie doll.
And silken robes make excellent
Tents in the garden. And when
Your nose itches, don't scratch it—
Pick it! Pick it! Pick it!
Lastly, remember:
Ain't never no such thing
As a life that's perfect in every way!
But faking it sure can be
Loads and loads of fun!
So pick it! Pick it! Pick it!

Aunt Castina came in from the kitchen and said, "I have a snack for you to travel with." She went around and handed each one of us a hard-boiled egg.

As she did this, I told the others, "An egg is a fine thing for traveling. It fits perfectly into the palm of your hand. And each one has its own sun inside. Now put the eggs someplace where they won't get crushed. Yolks can be sticky, you know."

We all thanked her very much, remembering politeness.

The phone rang, and Aunt Castina went to answer it. In a minute, she burst into the living room, her hands darting about her head like bats.

"My lands!" she exclaimed. "Oh, my word!" Aunt Castina did not handle surprise well.

"What is it, Aunt Castina?" asked Kenneth.

"That was Great-Gran at the hospital. They're releasing her right now! This changes our whole plan! Oh, Lordy!"

We ran around, getting wrapped and bundled. Aunt Castina muttered and mumbled to herself, trying to figure out a new plan.

"I'll have to bring you all to the bus station. That's what I'll do! I'll tell the taximan to wait. Rainie will see that . . . " She turned to me, "Rainie, you're to see that Louise and Little Belli get the bus. Now, your bus leaves at 9:47 and theirs leaves at 9:26." She was holding three separate bus schedules in her shaking hands, trying to figure out what to do.

It is a certain gift I have, that when someone becomes flustered, I become calm. I stood quietly and watched and listened, waiting for her to put me in charge of arrangements. Because that is what I do best. If Aunt Awful was smart, she would have known that by now.

She continued on in her rant, "Let's see, let's see. These schedules are so confusing. Now . . . 9:26. Yes! That'll work. Let me see, Rainie will help the girls find the bus, then Rainie can find Kenneth's bus to Poughkeepsie, then I'll take Baby Eddie . . . no! I can't handle him and Great-Gran, both! What to do? What to do? How am I ever going to manage this?"

Rainie Marie to the rescue, once more. I suggested that I would locate all buses for everyone. I would hold Baby Eddie while Aunt Castina and the taxi picked up Great-Gran at the hospital. Then Aunt Castina and Great-Gran would come back to the bus station, to see us off to our various destinations. I suggested this not only because it worked, but also because it might come in handy. I had an idea somewhere in the fog outside my brain. An idea that I thought might blossom into something very valuable. I

175

wasn't sure yet, but I felt that . . . maybe, just maybe . . .

I filled up the cat dishes with plenty of food, and we made our good-byes to Kit and Kat and Cynthia, and to the ghosts that kept Great-Gran's house in tune. I mentioned to the ghosts that they were doing a lousy job.

We piled into the taxi. The taximan stuffed our travel sacks into the trunk. Little Belli clung to Brown-Bear for dear life, and Kenneth to his Bible, and Samuel to his collage bag. Louise waved good-bye to her spider plant through the window, and through tears. I rubbed my acorn between my fingers frantically, trying to conjure up a moment of magic that would get us out of this taxi and into Mama's apartment back home.

The ride to the bus station was a silent one. Little Belli and Louise gripped each other's hands and huddled together. I saw Samuel squeeze Baby Eddie's chubby hand, then let go, as if he didn't want anyone to see he was emotional.

Little Belli and Baby Eddie both fit themselves into my lap. I was glad. The warmth from their bodies was something that I concentrated on all the way to the station. I needed to keep this remembrance for a long time. By the time I'd see them again, they might be too big for my lap. That thought clamped my heart down tight. I could hardly catch my breath. When we got to the bus station, Aunt Castina said to the taximan, "Wait here."

"It'll cost you, lady," he said gruffly. He was a Sunyellow taximan. I really had to talk to Great-Gran about the Sunyellow people.

Aunt Castina glared at him. He jerked back his head and sank into his seat and looked hard into his steering wheel.

"*Humph!*" said Aunt Castina.

We scurried in. People in the station turned to stare after us. We rattled through, all of us with our travel sacks bulging, a little girl with two heads—one girl head, one Brown-Bear head—a boy with a huge old leather Bible, another boy with a lumpy bag of collage supplies. Bits of colored paper trailed in a wild rainbow behind us.

We jostled each other over to the information booth and placed all our stuff on the floor around us. Aunt Castina glanced hurriedly at her watch.

"Oh, heavenly days," she exclaimed. "I've got to get to that hospital!"

She bent down, grabbed me by the shoulders, pulled me close, and said into my face, "You've got the tickets and the eggs and the food money I gave you?"

"Yes'm."

"Then you use this time to find out where the buses leave from and to say good-bye to your brothers and sisters."

The bus station went dim and fuzzy. My mouth felt jerked down. The inside of my nose got flooded.

"You're not going to cry, are you, Rainie Marie?" asked my aunt.

I shook my head no.

"Good girl," she told me. She stood up, went around, gave each of my brothers and sisters a sharp squeeze, and headed for the doors, her gray cloak swirling out around her. Then Aunt Castina turned back to me and called, "Rainie Marie Greene, I know you'll do the right thing."

The right thing, I thought, rubbing my

acorn. The right thing, I thought, looking around at the brothers and sisters. Yes, I will do the right thing.

Kenneth strolled over, hands in his pockets and trying to look cool, and said, "Wonder what the weather's like in Tennessee."

I mumbled, "There isn't any weather in Tennessee. It's just hot."

Samuel, scratching his head under his wool hat, began scanning the station floor for possible collage material. He said, "Wonder if they have litter in Tennessee."

"I wonder if we'll ever be together again," Louise said, and burst into tears. Again. Passersby, trying not to trip over our belongings strewn across the floor, looked at us as if they wondered which one of us had clobbered Louise hard enough to make her bawl so hard.

Samuel said, "Guess I better go get a drink of water. There's the fountain, way over there."

Kenneth followed him. They were both eager to leave the crying behind them. They stayed at the fountain until they saw that Louise had quieted down.

I told Louise to watch Little Belli and Baby Eddie, and then walked to the big sign that posted bus departures.

I turned to look back at the others, huddled together like sparrows in a storm. My aunt's words came back to me: "Rainie Marie Greene, I know you'll do the right thing."

What was the right thing? That idea still nudged at my mind. An answer. Some answer. It knocked and knocked at the door of my mind, but I couldn't find the key to unlock it.

And I feared the door would stay tight shut, until it was too late.

CHAPTER
EIGHTEEN

The door opened and the right thing jumped into my mind, just like that.

I grabbed Samuel by the sleeve and dragged him over to the information window.

"Sir? Sir?" I called up to the information man.

The man looked around but couldn't find me. I looked at the station clock. Time was running out!

"Sir!" I bellowed.

The information man looked down. He smiled. "What can I do for you, missy?"

"How far to the train station?"

"'Bout a ten-minute ride from here," he said, pointing the way.

Samuel grabbed me by my collar. "Train station! What are you doing?"

I ignored Samuel and asked the information man, "How long would that take to walk?"

He scratched his bald head. He leaned his elbows on the counter in front of him and said, "Oh, maybe half hour, I guess."

I yanked the tickets, all the tickets for everyone, out of my pocket. I pushed them at the information man.

"How much money would I get if I turned these tickets in?"

Samuel gasped and whispered in a choked voice, "Rainie Marie!"

The man scratched his head again and pulled out a thick book with names of cities and numbers and dollar signs in it. He shuffled through it, looking back and forth from the tickets to the book. He was extremely slow. Slow motion in my life—once again.

"Now . . . let . . . me . . . sssseeeeeee . . ."

"Please, mister, we're in a terrible hurry!" To Samuel, I said, "Go get the others."

"But . . ."

"No buts! Hurry!" I pushed him toward the little ones.

The information man said, "Let me sseeee . . .

$53.00 for each ticket to Tennessee . . . uhhh . . . 17.00 for Mahwah . . . $15.00 for Poughkeepsie, uhhh . . . tax . . . that comes to $166.92, little lady."

More than enough to get us all train tickets for home, back home to Mama! All of us! And Mama would even get money back! That'd make her happy.

"May I have the money, sir?" I asked, as politely as a person in a great hurry could ask.

"You have to go over to that window, missy. See that one over there, with the blond lady in it?"

I saw it, and I saw a long line of people waiting to buy tickets.

I said, "Thank you," signaled to Samuel to bring the others over to the window, and ran to the end of the line.

I called up all my courage and went to the man at the head of the line.

I said, "Excuse me, sir, I'm in a terrible hurry. May I cut in front of you?"

He was a skyscraper, this man. He curled his lips into a sneer, stuck up his nose, looked way, way down it at me, and said, "We are, all of us, in a hurry. And you, kid, must wait your turn."

I expected as much. I ran to the others and whispered my plan to them.

We all got at the end of the line in a ragged cluster and screamed at the tops of our lungs.

"I miss my mama!" screamed Kenneth.

"I gotta puke!" screamed Louise.

"I gotta go poop!" screamed Little Belli.

Samuel screeched, "Baby Eddie already went poop! Wanna smell?"

"*Yeeeeaaaaagggggghhhh!*" they all screamed together.

I let out my best, deepest, and most effective groan: "*Oooaaaahhhhuuuuuuu!*" and clutched at my belly.

Then we all burst into loud crocodile tears.

The people on line jumped into the air. They turned wildly around, as if looking for help. They held their ears, and their eyes popped out of their heads.

The blond lady behind the bars of the ticket window yelled, "Quiet down, please. Quiet down! Sir? Sir, would you pullleeeeaaassse let these chidren in front of you?"

"With pleasure!" he yelled back.

I exchanged the tickets for money, bundled the bills up, and stuck them way, way deep into my acorn pocket.

"Come with me," I shouted to my family.

We charged through the station doors, headed in the direction of the train station, when Samuel yelled at me, "What are we doing, Rainie Marie?"

I shouted back, "We are trampling down fierce lions and poisonous snakes! We are fighting the wind! We are doing the right thing!"

CHAPTER
NINETEEN

The first item on my agenda of escape was to call Mama with the news that her ducklings were about to return to their nest. As we marched toward the train station, I dug into the money envelope the bus station lady had given me. I scraped up all the change I had in my pockets, and went down the line of brothers and sisters, begging coins from them.

A telephone booth hung on a post on the corner of the street. I deposited money and dialed Mama's number.

"That is a long-distance call," said a taped operator voice. "Please deposit seventy-five cents for the first three minutes."

Three minutes was not much time to tell

Mama our future had been drastically changed. By me.

The phone rang only once, and Mama answered.

"Oh, Rainie Marie, I'm so lonely," she said.

"Mama, we're on our way home," I said.

"But, Rain, what about your trips to Tennessee and Mahwah and—"

"Never mind, Mama. I've taken care of everything, even Aunt Castina. Don't worry about a thing," I told her, hoping that my little lie about having already dealt with Aunt Castina would go unnoticed by the Higher Authority.

"Rainie Marie, what have you done? Rainie? . . ."

"Yes, Mama?"

"I'll be so happy to see you."

We made it to the train station in fifteen minutes, with Samuel, Kenneth, and me taking turns carrying Baby Eddie and Little Belli. The train station! And that familiar good old train that always took us to Great-Gran's, and always took us home again, would make one more trip for us.

We tore through the glass and brass doors and up to the ticket window, breathless. What luck—no lines!

"Five tickets to Poughkeepsie, please," I gasped.

"Yes, dear," said the ticket lady.

As she counted out the tickets, I asked, "When does the next train to Poughkeepsie leave?"

"Just left."

I could not have heard right. I said, "Excuse me?"

"Just left," she repeated.

Samuel asked, "When does the next one leave?"

"Not until tonight," said the lady.

My dream, my plan, went up in smoke.

"Here's your tickets," the woman said.

I shook my head. "Sorry for your trouble," I muttered, "but we don't need them anymore."

I plodded over to the bench in the station. It looked like a church pew, except that there was none of the comfort of church here for us. None of the hope.

Samuel said, "I told you so, Rainie Marie."

Kenneth said, "You should have done as you were told."

Louise, who never, ever said "shut up," said, "Shut up, both of you! Rainie Marie *was* doing as she was told. She was doing the right thing. She was trying to hold us together. Maybe that doesn't mean nothing to you, but it means plenty to us!"

"Yeah!" chimed in Little Belli. "Shut up!"

"What are we going to do now? We missed our buses. Aunt Awful will be back looking for us soon. She's gonna kill us," said Samuel.

"Not to mention what Great-Gran will do!" said Kenneth.

Louise said, "I think we gotta go back to the bus station." She put her hand on my shoulder and shook me gently. "Rainie Marie, think. Buses that take people to Tennessee and to Mahwah can take people to Poughkeepsie, too. Remember, Kenneth was going to Aunt Pludy's on a bus."

The trip back to the bus station, with our bags jiggling, the smile on Brown-Bear gleaming in the early sun, that trip was made on the wings of hope!

At the bus station, I walked up to the blond lady's window, which had no line now.

She looked down at me and said, "Oh."

I smiled my best smile at her. "Excuse me?"

She looked scared, as if to say, What do you have up your sleeve now? But instead she asked, "Yes?"

"When does the next bus leave for Poughkeepsie?"

She glanced at a printed pad in front of her and then at the clock on the wall. "You have nine minutes, honey."

"How much does a seventeen-month-old baby cost, for Poughkeepsie?"

She smiled. "If you keep the baby on your lap, nothing."

"Five bus tickets for Poughkeepsie, please," I said, loudly and clearly.

We found the bus and got on in just three minutes. We had six minutes to spare. All of a sudden, I thought—Aunt Castina will have a heart attack herself, when she comes back to the station and finds us gone! I grabbed a piece of paper and a crayon from Samuel's collage bag and wrote,

Dear Aunt Castina,
We have gone home to Mama.
We have traveled enough!
Sincerely,
Rainie Marie Greene

I jumped out of the seat. Samuel said, "Now what?"

"I'll be right back," I said, and jumped off the bus.

I ran to the information man and asked him, "Please, mister, give this to my aunt Castina when she comes. She'll be a tall lady in a silly cloak, looking for six kids."

While he was still mumbling, "Who? What? Where?" and scratching his bald head again, I ran back to the bus.

To the bus that was right now pulling away from its platform.

Through the bus windows, I saw the others waving their hands and pointing, their eyes big as blue moons, their mouths going faster than the wheels of the bus.

The bus picked up speed. In a second, it would leave the platform altogether, moving out onto the road. In a second, it would be too late.

I ran down the platform, along its very edge, waving my arms and screaming. I ran so fast, the edge of the platform went by in a blur.

"Hey! Hey! Wait for me!" I wrenched my throat out of joint, I screamed so loud.

Suddenly, the bus jerked to a stop. I'll never know if it stopped because the driver saw me running or if it stopped because of all the racket the little ones were making inside. Or if it stopped because the Mistress of Magic with her magic acorn willed it to stop.

The door sighed open. I scrambled up the big steps, thanked the bus driver most sincerely, and fell into my seat beside Louise and Little Belli.

I looked at them, took their hands in mine, grinned at the boys, and said, "The last travel with Rainie Marie. Next station stop—home."